I0452128

Making Lemonade

Making Lemonade is a remarkable anthology that tackles difficult topics with honesty and courage. The passionate storytellers of Canvey Writers have created a passionate collection that tackles the painful realities of mental health struggles, but also celebrates resilience and the power of community. Making Lemonade inspires understanding, empathy and comfort to those who may feel alone in their battles.

Jonathan Phang Writer,
TV presenter, photographer and cook

I have just stood up from my desk and given Canvey Writers a round-of applause.

Peter Holland,
Media Manager PAPYRUS

Making Lemonade

A Short Novel by Canvey Writers

In celebration of their tenth birthday

Edited by Debz Hobbs-Wyatt

All profits will be donated to the charity – *PAPYRUS*

Bridge House

This collection copyright © Bridge House 2025.
Copyright in the text reproduced herein remains the property
of the individual authors, and permission to publish is
gratefully acknowledged by the editors and publishers.

All rights reserved

No parts of this publication may be reproduced, stored in a
retrieval system, or transmitted in any form or by any
means, electronic, mechanical, photocopying, recording or
otherwise without prior permission of the copyright owner.

British Library Cataloguing in Publication Data

A Record of this Publication is available from the British
Library

ISBN 978-1-917854-08-5

This edition published 2025 by Bridge House Publishing
Manchester, England

Our aim is to let fiction – that can too cruelly mimic real events – raise a much-needed awareness about the things facing young people today.

Contents

Introduction

I am an award-winning short story writer and agented published novelist. I am also the founder and chair of a small writing group called Canvey Writers, based in Essex, on Canvey Island. It's a small island in the Thames estuary, forty miles from London.

Some time ago I had an idea for a collaborative writing project for the group to write about characters on a fictitious street. I first proposed it during lockdown when we came together on Zoom. However, polarised by world events at the time, it somehow got hijacked and turned into a crime novel related to a virus and a plot to infect the world! This is what happens when you get lots of creative people together in the middle of a pandemic! And it turns out writing and plotting a crime novel with twelve or more separate voices – as a group – was far too complicated, so we sadly abandoned it. But a valuable writing lesson was learned.

A couple of years later, having already published an anthology of work some years ago, and with the group keen to work together again, I proposed we return to the idea of the street. I told people to think about Alan Bennett's fantastic *Talking Heads* series where people told their own stories, using humour, poignancy and pathos. So, can you create a character on a street, I asked, let's say a fictitious suburb of London, and tell their story *Talking Heads* style? So, in essence everyone was to write a character's story as a chapter. In first person it means you hear different voices, some can be present tense, some past tense, that was their choice.

Woven between the lines and as a thread through the story is another story, the real story, the story that arcs through the book. So now they had to learn about how novels work too, so this is a short story collection and a novel in one. Remember – we're a writing group and since I am also a writing coach, editor and mentor, it was about pushing boundaries and learning how stories work to get the message across in the most engaging and effective way.

The premise is this: something terrible happened on Station Square. The story deals with the ripple effects of that on all of their lives. It's a story about something that could have, and actually has, happened to real people.

What started out as an experimental writing project quickly became something else and almost two years later, working on this alongside our own projects, and with critiquing sessions and offering valuable feedback to one another, we turned it into something far more important. In fact, we came to realise the true power of fiction for raising awareness – even with subject matters people often don't like to talk about. In here you will meet people with all kinds of issues to deal with from mental illness to dementia to hoarding. These are people of all ages and from different backgrounds. But the real story is that of a young girl we called Joanne and how what happened to her impacted on the people living close by, some more so than others, as would be the case in real life.

Without meaning to sound patronising, I am so proud of what my writers achieved because some had never been published, some were new to writing – and we had to work hard **all together** to refine and develop these stories. I pushed them because we needed to get this right. What also became quickly apparent was just how emotionally invested everyone became in this story... and how much they believed in getting its much-needed message out into the world. For this reason, we approached a charity that we felt we needed to learn from and work with to ensure we handle sensitive subject matter with the understanding it truly needs.

And this little book is the result. I was thrilled that Bridge House Publishing, who I share a long association with, especially with charity books, said a resounding YES to publishing it. It's got a message we believe needs to be heard. We want it to be read by adults and young adults alike, and have included some discussion points at the end because we think this is more than just a story…

So please sit back and enjoy the work of the Canvey Writers. And afterwards please do us a favour and consider buying an extra copy and donating it to your local secondary school or youth group, even ask your library to stock it. We rely on word of mouth to ensure the book does what we sincerely hope it will and needs to do. Thank you so much.

Debz Hobbs-Wyatt
Author – Editor – Chair of Canvey Writers

Station Square

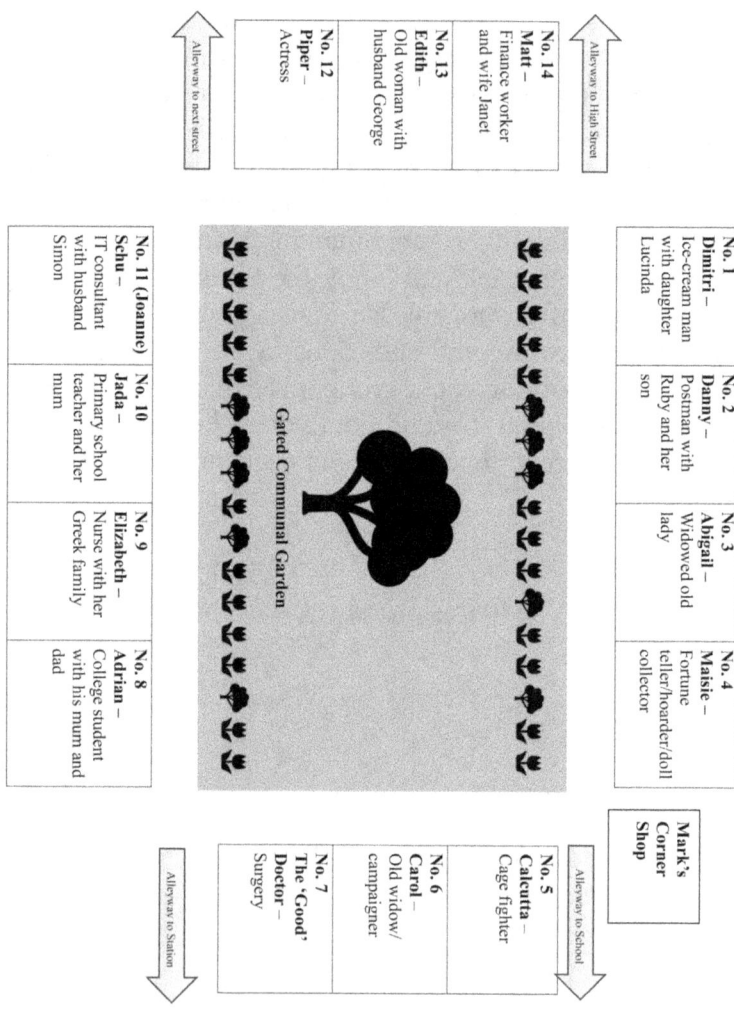

Alleyway to High Street

No. 14
Matt – Finance worker and wife Janet

No. 13
Edith – Old woman with husband George

No. 12
Piper – Actress

Alleyway to next street

No. 1
Dimitri – Ice-cream man with daughter Lucinda

No. 2
Danny – Postman with Ruby and her son

No. 3
Abigail – Widowed old lady

No. 4
Maisie – Fortune teller/hoarder/doll collector

Gated Communal Garden

No. 11 (Joanne)
Schu – IT consultant with husband Simon

No. 10
Jada – Primary school teacher and her mum

No. 9
Elizabeth – Nurse with her Greek family

No. 8
Adrian – College student with his mum and dad

Alleyway to Station

Mark's Corner Shop

Alleyway to School

No. 5
Calcutta – Cage fighter

No. 6
Carol – Old widow/campaigner

No. 7
The 'Good' Doctor – Surgery

"People never notice anything."
        — **J.D. Salinger, The Catcher in the Rye**

Or do they?

Prologue

October 13th

Who wants flowers when you're dead?

Sometimes the last book we read. the last TV show we watched. the last thoughts we had have a way of staying with us. You'd been reading *The Catcher in the Rye*. They found it amongst your things. The bookmark a few pages from the end. You never got to know how it ended. There's something truly heartbreaking about that: about unfinished moments, like unspent coins in a purse, unturned pages on a calendar, unspoken words on lips.

It's true – flowers are wasted on the dead just as youth is wasted on the young.

There would have been flowers for you last year – there are always flowers.

My fingers bend over the edges of the page – marking the place. They want me to say a few words. They want me to make sense of something broken.

The voices soften to an almost-whisper without anyone saying a word. People have a way of sensing things. The old woman, Maisie, in the bright colours, gypsy-like, seems to sense it first. She stops mid-sentence. She's been talking to Abigail, probably telling her about her latest charity-shop acquisition: another doll she told me earlier. I wonder if she'll tell her the part about how the hair being blonde and the eyes being blue reminded her of you.

She stops talking right there in the middle of all the bustle in the communal garden and gestures for Abigail to follow her to the rows of chairs. They're lined up in front on a make-shift "stage" area. Just along from the tree; the silver birch that stands alone showing off its overcoat,

14

leaves predominantly oranges and browns but still retaining some green. It stands as if in salute for what is about to happen. Harriet Smallcroft, our local MP, will say something first. The other speakers are here. I see them talking to people. It's a nice day for it, people say. And I know what they mean but is it, can it ever be, a nice day for it? There are clear blue skies, a day with crispy edges, but there's a chill stirring the leaves of the silver birch – a chill that runs through everything.

Not everyone's here yet.

Earlier Carol, she's the one who sent out the invites, the one who'll also speak today, was with Maisie and Abigail; they were sweeping leaves. I joined them. They said they *were* going to make cakes and sausage rolls and the WI wanted to help serve refreshments but Carol was the one who said it wasn't that *kind of thing.* They didn't need to make refreshments and what if it rained? It's not about food or drink, is it, it's about all being here.

So, we are.

We are all here.

There are a lot of people. We're all here huddled in our winter coats. Hats and scarves, stomping our feet to keep warm. Carol asked me to be here. I don't know how to answer all their questions.

I spoke to Edith earlier. Another old neighbour. She's here with her husband George though she says he probably doesn't really understand what today is. Made me realise how we're all fighting our own battles. Edith is making her way to the front now to join Piper – Piper Marigold the actress – I recognise her from the paper. Today it seems she's sitting alone with her head bowed. She looks glamorous in a long burgundy coat with a gold scarf. Her hair has grown since I last saw her photo. Calcutta Drake's here too. The MMA fighter. He's brought his black labrador along with him, the one you used to walk. He's not exactly sociable but he did tell me about your walks. He's sitting at the end of one of the rows. He feels it too; I see it in his anguished expression when he shifts his gaze from his knees, as if he's wondering who else will come. He looks as if he's expecting trouble. Always ready for a fight, I suppose. I did see him dip his head at Danny the postman, at least I think that's who he is. I think it was Jada, the teacher, who told me that. He was hovering by the gate, but I don't see him now. I look along the lines of young faces and I feel something stir.

They all carry a small part of what happened – young and old – and I see the way it adds weight to their smiles and droops their shoulders.

The press is here too, gathered at the edges with their notebooks and their phones; some with cameras. I hope they're here for the right reasons. This is not about headlines and click-baits.

We are here for you.

I find my seat on the makeshift stage and look over at Harriet Smallcroft who is yet to take her position. The hush sweeps over heads and pushes their whispers into the corners of the kempt garden. I watch a solitary leaf fall from the silver birch and float gently to the ground.

And that thing – the thing that had hung between their words and their handshakes and their slightly nervous banter a few moments ago, rises like bubbles to the surface of a glass.

We're nearly ready.

Jada – with her gorgeous braided hair – now raises her hands, ushering more people to take their seats. She also seems to be looking around. Checking if everyone came, I suppose. I see Elizabeth the lovely Greek lady. She lived next-door-but-one to you. She says she's known you since you were a baby. The whole family is here, sitting right down at the front across from me; young people you used to play with. She has left four seats empty. Carol wrote them a letter. Elizabeth has spoken to them and so did I – but will they come? Will they be *able* to come?

Behind Elizabeth, I see the two Simons looking very serious in smart grey suits – matching. They were involved in publicising the event. I wonder how they feel living at number 11. Then there's Adrian who said you were close friends. He's sitting in the fourth row with his mum and dad and there are so many people I haven't yet spoken to. Dimitri, the ice cream man, who I do know, is sitting with his daughter, Lucinda, right behind Adrian. I see the boy turn around and glance at her. Something seems to pass between them that makes me wonder. It's like they've found some solace in one another remembering you. Adrian's lips are pressed into a tight line, expression fixed, stoic and I watch Lucinda lean forward and gently squeeze his shoulder.

I have spoken to as many of them as I can.

Now it feels like a play is about to start. I wish that's all today was.

You asked Adrian to keep your words safe. I feel the weight of those words now – of the responsibility handed to me.

Harriet Smallcroft fiddles with a microphone and taps the end once and then again to make sure. She looks at her wrist, glances at me and mouths, "Give it another minute?" I nod but the second I do, I catch a glimpse of them – so they did make it. It seems all heads turn and all gazes follow them as they make their way to the front – a mother, a father, a grandfather, a brother; all in their winter coats. I see Jada turn to look at the boy, Jimmy. Abigail nods at the old man. They shuffle into the seats Elizabeth saved for them. Now Harriet Smallcroft smiles in their direction. I can only imagine how they all feel.

I sense movement at the back: a man in a suit wearing a black tie. I think that's the doctor from the old surgery on the corner. He's standing by the railing with an older couple who I believe are an aunt and uncle. But I still don't see *him*.

We're about ready to start.

Today is important and that's why there are so many people here: many of your friends from school and teachers and even the headmaster from Crompton Seniors.

There's a sense of shifting feet and poised cameras as the press make ready. Harriet stands more upright now and begins her short introduction and the whole time I'm thinking about what to say, how to start. But I know. There's only one way to start.

I look out at the sea of scarves and hats and solemn faces while Harriet talks about how it's one year since the terrible tragedy... I try not to look at the family, not yet.

When finally, I hear myself being introduced, I stand, brush down my suit and I walk to the microphone. I see hope in all their expectant stares, like they need me to make sense of it – even when I know that's impossible.

My fingers tremble as I open the page to the right place. I'm doing this for you – because you can't and I wish to God I didn't have to. I stare down at the neat black handwriting with the dainty loops and the slight lean to the right. There's a soft muffle of hand taps as if they don't know if they ought to clap or not. Now the hush returns.

"Hello. I want to begin with something Joanne Wilson wrote in her diary…"

I see their faces fixed on me, draw in a deep breath and begin.

"When I was a little girl, I had an idea that I'd make my own lemonade. I'd use fresh lemons – and mix them with sugar and water. Then I'd fill glass jugs and sell it by the cup. I'd do it during the summer holidays on the square. Only I never did do it because I used to be so shy and there were always too many other things to do with the school holidays."

Your mum raises her head. I did ask her if I could do this and she gave me her blessing.

That's when I think I see movement at the back by the railing and adjust my gaze.

He came.

He's standing right at the back.

He's here.

I look back down at the page and continue.

"I always wanted to be that little girl who made lemonade. I always wanted to be noticed."

I see the gravitas of your words on their faces, think how there are many ways to be noticed – but this is not the way.

"Nothing will ever make it right – what happened," I say, and I wonder for a moment as I look out at all the faces here today on the square, what you would make of all this, of all of these people here – now – for you.

Then I draw in a deep breath and I continue.

The Secret Diary of Joanne Wilson –
aged 14 years, 3 months

I don't care if it's a sad good-bye or a bad good-bye, but when I leave a place, I like to know I'm leaving it.
— **J.D. Salinger, The Catcher in the Rye**

Today wasn't a "good-bye" but a "hello". Jack asked me out after Biology class!

One Year Ago

October
Number 10
Jada

I never thought we would end up here – in this beautiful square. Or that when I'd only been here a few months something truly terrible would happen right next door.

Station Square is a lovely place to live, despite what happened. It's so different to the tiny little flat we had on the fifth floor of a tower block in Hackney. As I close the front door and step into the street, the cold October breeze steals my breath. I'm debating whether to do this run, but I know I'll feel better afterwards. I cross the road and enter the communal garden. The grass is covered in a thick frost that looks like delicate lace; it looks so different now. When Mum and I first viewed the house back in early spring, the daffodils looked like beautiful yellow trumpets announcing new life, but they have disappeared along with the vibrant red tulips. Back then the trees wore various shades of green and the shrubs were thick with foliage. That big tree, the silver birch, was awash with catkins. Now the autumn has returned and the leaves are falling. The scene is like an abstract painting of rustic colour. Though the silver birch has lost most of its green it still commands a presence.

When we first viewed the house, I remembered that as we approached the steps to number 10 Station Square, I first saw little Jimmy. He was at the window next door and as I looked up at him, he poked his tongue out at me. He looked so cute with beautiful auburn hair and little cheeky dimples.

I had no idea when I took the job at Crompton Primary, that he would end up in my class.

Mum decided that day, as soon as she walked through the door, that the house was exactly what she wanted to spend her inheritance money on – even if it did need a ton of work. We had to wait a while before we could move in, but we could see the potential. As soon as the offer was accepted, and we got the keys, Mum got workmen in to do all the repairs, and to decorate. I was relieved when we could finally move in and I could start work at Crompton Primary.

I love my new job and getting to know the twenty-eight pupils in my class. I know I shouldn't have favourites, but Jimmy was funny – six going on sixteen. As I walked into the classroom and introduced myself last month, he recognised me from being the lady he poked his tongue out at. I'm guessing he might have seen us coming and going as we got the house ready over the summer, though I hadn't seen him – or anyone at number 11 for that matter. He was the life and soul of the classroom. He chatted and laughed a lot, which made all the children gravitate towards him. I often had to reprimand his behaviour because the more the other children laughed at his antics, the more he showed off. I thought he could have a career as a comedian. I overheard him telling his little girlfriend Daisy that when he went on holiday on an airplane that he told his sister to keep her seatbelt on in case the pilot had to brake sharp.

That was the first time I heard that he had a sister. That did make me laugh. He also said that he wanted to buy Daisy a puppy for her birthday; he needed £6 and he only had £3 pocket money saved up. He loved painting, especially animals. I asked him if he had any pets and he said, "No, but my sister Joanne walks a dog."

It seems like it happened more than a week ago – the

23

thing – that's how people refer to it. Or "the terrible thing" like it's too hard to say the words. The spring sunshine chased away by the autumn gloom.

The run is extremely hard this morning; I was hoping to at least do my usual five miles but it's so cold out I only do a couple. En route I have to pass Mark's shop on the corner that's been selling Halloween stuff for weeks. A skeleton swaying in the wind hanging from the awning, a witch's broomstick balancing from wire in the window. Pumpkins everywhere, door wreaths with golden fake leaves and owls, displayed on a trolley. I wanted to find out how I could decorate the square for Halloween when I first saw it. I thought the children would love it, but it wouldn't be appropriate now, would it? Not after what happened last week.

The cold air steals my breath as I return to the square, so I decide to sit on a bench even though I can see it's damp from the morning dew. My legs are jelly. I look across the gardens where Mum is on the step, putting the key in the door. She's just got home from doing a night shift at the hospital. I see her hesitate to look down at the flowers and candles on the pavement outside number 11. It must bring it all back for her too as it does for me. Reminding both of us of another day that changed *our* lives.

I miss Dad so much; I loved his long dreadlocks and his beautiful green eyes. The way he always said, "Hello, my Jada, my precious girl." He wasn't just my dad, but my best friend, my hero.

I remember Jimmy saying Joanne was his sister but also his best friend when he did a painting of her one day in class. What I could make out of the painting was her wearing a school uniform and carrying a book in her stick-thin hand. I asked him if it was her schoolbook and he said,

24

"No it's her diary. She had a row with Mummy so she took the diary with her to school, so Mummy wouldn't read it."

"Is that why Joanne has a sad face in the picture?"

"Yes." He looked solemnly at the painting.

I wonder what happened to that diary?

I stood holding his hand, waiting for someone to collect him from school that day – *the* day. The day last week when the terrible thing happened to him, though it hasn't only happened to him or his family, has it? I feel that as sure as the seasons change, so will all of us – in one way or the other. I might not have lived on the square for long or known the family for any length of time, but time in moments like these always feels so transient, doesn't it?

When nobody came, I took Jimmy to the head's office, and she phoned Jimmy's mother. Mrs Wilson explained that Joanne should have collected him from school, as they were out shopping, but they would be there as soon as possible. I took Jimmy back to our classroom to wait for them and gave him some squash and a biscuit, and we started doing a puzzle. We waited for quite a while before both Mr and Mrs Wilson arrived, looking flustered. They were apologetic and said they had tried ringing Joanne, but she hadn't answered her phone. That maybe she'd been asked to stay late at school. Something in their expressions made me think that wasn't the first time. Teenagers, eh? Lose track of time. I'm sure I saw her once with a boyfriend. How easily they get distracted. Of course, the Wilsons recognised me right away as their new neighbour and I did say if it happened again, I could always bring Jimmy home if they signed a permissions slip to say... only I never finished saying it because they seemed eager to leave. I didn't take it personally. I could see they were concerned about Joanne. And they didn't really know me, did they?

What I couldn't have known, what none of us could ever have known in that moment was the real reason Joanne didn't come to collect Jimmy that day.

I was surprised when Jimmy's grandad brought him to the school this week. I guess they didn't know what to do and he'd said he wanted to come. It's a distraction, I guess. He asked me if I could keep my eye on him and said he thought it would be better for him to be here with his school friends than being at home for the next couple of days, whilst they sorted out the funeral arrangements. I tried to say something meaningful but the words died on my lips. Of course I would look out for him. What those poor parents must have been going through.

Jimmy was fine until the children started asking him about his sister. Mason asked him, "What happened then? Was it an accident? Was it her fault?"

Jimmy shouted at Mason to shut up, then the tears came. I took Jimmy to our wellbeing room. I could empathise with how he felt. Grief is a weird thing; it's a block of every emotion you have. Fear, guilt, sadness, anger. It must be even worse for a six-year-old who doesn't understand. How can he? Will he ever?

"Miss, where do people go when they die?"

"Well..." *how do you even answer that?* "... People think you go to a place called heaven."

He seemed to think about that and I could see his thoughts ticking over.

"Does the Number 17 bus go there? I'll ask Grandad to take me."

"Let's go back to class and you can do some painting," I said as I put my hand on his shoulder and walked him out into the corridor. Not many children leave me lost for words. Now wouldn't a bus to heaven be a nice idea.

26

"What shall I paint, Miss?" He looked up at me with his sad blue eyes.

"Anything you like, Jimmy. Anything at all."

As I look at my Fitbit, I have done just over five thousand steps and my heart rate's one hundred and twenty-seven beats per min. That will do for today; I've got to save some energy for later as I have promised Mum to help with the garden this afternoon. We have bought a beautiful pot for a Dracaena tree for Dad. Its common name is "Song of Jamaica". We thought this would be appropriate as he was a Jamaican musician. I wonder if they will plant a tree for Joanne? Maybe they'll be more sensible and do it when the earth is softer, like in the spring, though.

As I stand up from the cold hard bench, rubbing off the winter debris from my leggings, I notice an elderly lady peering at me from behind the curtain of number 4. She looks so sad. I proffer a slight wave and attempt a smile. She hesitates before she lifts her hand and then she turns away. I will make a point of getting to know my new neighbours but now is not the right time. As I cross the gardens towards number 11, I see Carol from number 6.

"Morning, Jada. Bit cold for a run today," she says, pulling the collar of her coat up to her ears. I look at the tealight she's clasping.

"I'm just going to light this for Joanne," she says. "It's so sad especially for little Jimmy. How do they cope in school with things like this happening?"

"They have a wellbeing room in most schools. We have one and they have one in Crompton Seniors too where the children can go and talk to someone about their feelings, or to just sit in a quiet place. Joanne's friends will have been counselled."

"I feel I need to do something to help," Carol says,

looking tearful as she places the candle on the pavement outside number 11. There are so many now. Though I've not seen the family. The curtains are closed.

"I think we all feel like that, Carol." I look down at all the flowers and teddies. I leave Carol fumbling with the lighter and the tealight.

I thought Carol was a nosy neighbour at first because the day we moved in she was straight over knocking on the door, but as it turned out she was delivering a homemade shepherd's pie to welcome us. We didn't invite her in then as there were boxes everywhere, but we have since become quite friendly and she is the only neighbour we've talked to so far.

As I step inside our home, I meet Mum in the hallway. She's holding supermarket carnations in cellophane and a tealight.

"Morning, Jada, how was your run?"

"Hard this morning, but I managed two miles. It's so cold."

"I'm surprised you went. Anyway, I think we should place these next door, don't you?"

"Yes."

It's not really the way you want to know the neighbours, or become part of the square, is it?

"Then we can have a cuppa together before I go to bed for a few hours and hopefully by the time we pot Dad's tree this afternoon it might be a bit warmer."

I think about the couple of times I saw Joanne when she picked Jimmy up from school and how excited he was to see her. Everyone says good things about her. It's a pity I never got to know her.

What a tragedy, a life cut down in its prime.

As I light the candle its flame bends over in the wind, and I set it down gently on the ground. As I stand, a tear escapes and dribbles along my cheek. That's when Mum reaches for my hand.

I pray that the family will heal with time.

I pray that little Jimmy will be okay, that he'll recover from this.

The shock is fresh. Will it ever pass?

And as I think about Dad's Song of Jamaica plant, I pray that we'll be okay too and that Dad will make sure Joanne has arrived safely. Wherever that is.

I think for a moment, as Mum's hand tightens over mine, *if only* there's a heaven. *If only* the Number 17 bus goes up that way, even for a brief visit. And *if only* Joanne had realised how much she had to live for.

The Secret Diary of Joanne Wilson – aged 14 years, 3 months and 1 week

It always smelled like it was raining outside, even if it wasn't, and you were in the only nice, dry, cosy place in the world.
— **J.D. Salinger, The Catcher in the Rye**

My cosy place... being kissed by Jack in the rain. I am supposed to be finishing my history project but I can't stop thinking about Jack.

November
Number 4
Maisie

They know me at the charity shop. They're my friends.

Mostly, I like buying dolls. Baby-faced ones with cute rosebud mouths. Every day at ten, I'm a creature of habit you see. I collect my trolley from behind the front door and make my way to the high street.

I dress for the occasion. A colourful long skirt, red blouse and green shawl with beaded gold trim. I wear a turban I've made myself from one of my many sparkly scarves. It's on account of having unruly hair to tame.

Sometimes at the charity shop, they make tea and serve it in real porcelain cups, then they say, "Read our leaves, Maisie."

So, I take their cups and swill them round and tell them what I can see. A marriage. A windfall. A birth. Nothing nasty you understand. If I see anything nasty, I keep it to myself 'cause once seen and told, it can't ever be avoided, no matter what.

If I find a new doll, I hug her close and whisper, "You can come home with me."

Joanne used to like my dolls. She'd knock on my door after school and say, "Any new babies, Maisie?"

She'd come right in and we would line them up to give them names and lives and stories to tell.

When Joanne grew older, the knocking stopped. Once, when she walked on by, I banged on the window and held up a new doll. She turned and smiled. Then shrugged and carried on. I heard her answer on the wind, "I'm too old for dolls."

There on the corner was the boy who always waited, leaning against the wall, all casual like.

Abigail is round at mine. Came knocking early. She misses her Terry so much. I know she would like me to read the leaves, tell her what she wants to hear. Tell her he is happy wherever he is but that's not what I do. So I say, "Let him rest in peace, Abbey."

Then I pour the tea and she settles and we chat about ordinary things. Only things aren't ordinary anymore.

Not since what happened to Joanne.

Abigail drains her cup and stares at the leaves. She says, "Did you see it, Maisie? In the leaves I mean?"

I nod, the smallest of nods and murmur under my breath, "Once seen and told, it can't ever be avoided."

Somewhere in the distance an early firework sounds. Bubbles, his whiskers twitching, looks up at me then scampers under the table to hide.

"No fireworks this year in the square, no celebrations," Abigail says.

Then she shivers and I pass her one of my shawls and we sit in our sparkles in companiable silence and try and remember happier times.

Abigail has gone home so I look at all my treasures. Not a spare square of floor space to be had but that's the way I like it.

Council 'as come knocking again. They're shouting through the letterbox. "You're a fire hazard, Miss Patterson. We've had complaints about your hoarding."

I shout back, "Bugger off."

That sorts them.

I listen as their footsteps retreat and then I remember.

The circus top, me flying the trapeze as free as a bird, all dressed in pink sparkles and white feathers with my unruly hair tight inside a sparkly turban. I can hear the applause and see the upturned faces of the audience like china dolls with round rosebud mouths open in awe. So I climb to reach the top shelf and my dolls and—

Blasted leg.

I shouldn't have climbed.

The street lights are shining on Bubbles washing his whiskers ignoring me on the floor, my new doll lying cold, just out of reach. Her white china face with its blue eyes pleading and red rosebud mouth calling.

Perhaps I should call out too. Perhaps then I would be sitting in my chair, cup of warm milk in my hand. No matter, I'll just lie here a little longer.

Leg is numb. Damn leg.

The fireworks are still sounding in the distance.

But not on Station Square.

I imagine people standing in huddled groups outside whispering about what happened and me with my trolley, slipping silently past, head bowed en route to see my friends.

At the shop they will say, "Maisie, did you see it in the tea leaves?"

I'll shake my head and tell them what they want to hear.

Then smiling, they'll bring out their best porcelain cups and go back to their untroubled lives.

The yellow street light has gone and I watch the dust dancing in a beam of sunlight shining through the glass in the door.

I can't feel my leg now and still my new doll lies just out of reach, her round rosebud mouth calling soundlessly.

Knocking again, then the letterbox opens. "Maisie, are you there?" A pair of eyes peer through the letterbox and the voice says, "It's me, your friend from the shop. We have a new doll. We missed you this morning."

I call out, my voice barely a whisper sounds loud in my head. "Yes, damn leg, it's let me down."

The letterbox slams shut and footsteps start to run and fade as they retreat down the path.

I must've dozed. In the gloom I see a face, a kindly face, looking down. I peer and see a burly policeman, his cap at a jaunty angle squeezing past my treasures. Behind him, my friend from the shop; her brow furrowed, her smile gone. She clutches a doll close.

Bubbles appears and meows hungrily, rubbing himself against my leg and a police radio crackles into life. I watch as a blue light from an ambulance flickers through the coloured glass of the door.

At the charity shop they're waiting. New porcelain cups and a fancy teapot full of real tea.

"Glad to have you back, Maisie."

Then they pour and we drink. I take their cups and swill them round and tell them what I can see.

A marriage. A windfall. A birth.

The Secret Diary of Joanne Wilson – aged 14 years, 4 months and 2 days

The terrible thing about dying is that you can only do it once.

— The Doctor in *Dr Who*, BBC

Joanne 4 Jack
Today we watched Dr Who together. He says he loves me. Do I deserve him?

December
Number 9
Elizabeth

December, and the sun is out in all its glory. A crisp cold winter's day. I sit in the conservatory, cup of coffee in one hand, biscuit in the other. A box of decorations on the table, the Christmas tree still in its red bag. Hubby brought it down from the loft last week but I just don't have the heart to do it – not yet. While they're all out Christmas shopping, I did say I'd make a start.

Five more minutes.

When something terrible happens we have to carry on but how can we?

The wall on the south side of the house is like a suntrap and the sunrays wash over you when you sit there enjoying the day. Or try to. It's hard to enjoy anything after what happened to that poor girl next door but one.

I watch two wood pigeons chasing each other over a few seeds. The sunflower seeds in the shell hanging from the apple tree for the small birds, leaves plenty on the ground for the wood pigeons. I watch them early in the morning with the typical strange movement of their heads as they trot back and forth on the fence. I feel they must have some tune in their mind as they move in a rhythmic way. Hector our golden retriever often chases them but today even he feels the sadness in the house. He is resting his head on his front paws and watches them as they enjoy the free meal.

Our old Victorian house, built early in the century, overlooks the communal garden.

The house has been renovated with love and brought

into the twenty-first century, without spoiling the original features that attracted us to it in the first place.

High ceilings with big windows make the house homely and full of light. The logs on the fires in the open fireplaces in our two living rooms in winter is where dreams are made. Weekends are special with the kids.

Years ago, houses were built with families in mind. Solid interesting places that people, once settled, very rarely sold. Our house is the place we want to be while the children are growing and have space to feel comfortable.

When you have three children: a boy and two girls, and a golden retriever, life is never dull.

I am of Pontian Greek origin. Pontiacs are the Greeks who lived in North Turkey since the Argonauts travelled to the Black Sea for the Golden Fleece. Obviously, many followed in a great migration.

I am here today because of what I learned from strong Greek women who gave me the mental capacity to survive dealing with people's grief. I just don't feel very strong today. My eyes wander back to the box on the table. They'll be home soon. I'll make the most of the quiet for a little longer.

I came to the UK for a few years to study for a Cambridge certificate which would qualify me to teach English back home. As I had to finance it myself for my studies I started doing nursing in a small hospital in Essex. Nursing is a profession which if you grow to like, you become hooked. I feel that is a job worth doing, tiring but fulfilling. I never went back. Sometimes it feels like Station Square has always been my home. Though the memories are never far away.

Christmas means people are busy buying presents for

family and friends, but all I can think is it's so unfair what happened to Joanne. Earlier I was at the front window, looking over at the communal garden, at the big tree. A few short weeks ago it was a glorious blend of golden reds and greens. Now the leaves gone, its branches bare. The cycle of life. This year leaves shed like tears that no one wants to sweep away. Made me realise how seasons change and life goes on while for some it's over.

My nana, who was a very religious woman, always said that God had a plan for all of us.

I still wonder what God's plan was for the Wilsons on that chilly October evening a few weeks ago when time seemed to stand still for our dear friends. It was a day which shook the quiet neighbourhood. I can't imagine something so tragic happening to one of our children.

Joanne Wilson took her own life.

The Wilsons moved into number 11, when young Joanne was just a baby. It was a few weeks before Christmas and Joanne, a pretty infant, was carried by her mum in a pink blanket. The weather turned early that year, and we had already started with some logs on our fire to warm our sitting rooms. The kids loved listening to the crackling of the flames and the smell of the wood burning. There is something magical about an open fire in a comfortable room embracing a family in the evenings.

We offered for Mrs Wilson – Evelyn – to bring the baby in as their house was cold and there was a problem with the heating. We prepared lunch and invited them to join us. Our kids were young then. Our first one five and our girl two; they grew up with Joanne and became close friends. Our second daughter was born when Joanne was four.

I love making my Greek cakes and sweets and the

Wilsons surely have a sweet tooth! They are a friendly and loving family and with Evelyn we had a good laugh while the kids were playing; caught up with the week's happenings. The men watched their football in the other room. Evelyn always told us stories about her grandfather who was a jolly man, and I told her stories about mine. My old grandpa liked a bit of ouzo because it was the manly thing for the Greek old men!

He had to see a young doctor once as he was getting a bit dizzy at times. The doctor suggested that he stopped drinking as he had hypertension. When he returned home my mother wanted to know what the doctor told him. He just said he needed a soup bowl. My mum fetched the deep bowl and in amazement watched her father pouring the drink into the bowl and carried on dipping his bread in the drink and eating it. "Well," he said, "the doctor said not to drink it; he never said not to eat it."

Evelyn laughed so much that day, that the men came in the dining room to find out what it was all about.

My thoughts are wandering back to the past – which they so often do. It helps, you know, because if I think about what it must be like for that poor family now, I will crumble. For them this time of the year will never be the same, will it? And I really should start on the tree before they all come home. Because we are all still here and we must remember that. My gran would say dead with dead and living with living. Although my mother said often, "The old girl lost it when her sister passed during her second pregnancy."

Life. Goes. On. Because it must.

In the past, if I didn't have to work on any of the Christmas evenings, we had a gathering of friends and neighbours. The Wilsons were our choice of friends. They had their little boy Jimmy, six years ago; he was a delight to look after when they needed support.

Joanne would pick up our Christmas cards for the neighbours as she was posting theirs. She was always ready to help.

My mind travels back to when our kids were playing in this garden wetting each other with the hose and chasing Joanne, giggling in the warm sun.

Joanne was a lovely quiet girl – blonde with blue smiling eyes like a summer's sea. You felt you could look into her innocent soul.

She was about five years younger than our son Chris and there was a couple of years between Joanne and our oldest daughter Silvy. Our youngest, Denise was always in awe of her. She liked playing with her blonde hair. Denise being nine years younger than Chris was seen as a nuisance and often the older ones would lock her out of the room where they played board games.

Joanne often stayed with us when her parents needed to go on a day out on their own. On the way home from Crompton Seniors, Joanne sometimes rang the bell for a chat with the kids and when they were not back from their school, we would chat and drink tea. She did not like going in the house if her mother was not at home. She loved our Helleborus plants in winter in our garden, amazed how some plants survived the cold and snow. My husband divided the plants this summer and gave them to Joanne for their garden; she will never see them flowering now, will she?

The day it happened I was on a busy night shift. Unusually, I'd gone in straight from meeting an old friend that afternoon so I'd not even been home. My phone had died and I didn't get the chance to charge it, so I didn't even see all the missed calls or know about the voicemails from them. But there they were – my family the following morning waiting for me even before my key was in the front door. No smiles, just red eyes, and no one could look straight into my face. Hubby ushered me in, asking why I hadn't picked up, because they had something to tell me. Even Hector went and slept near the fireplace. He behaved strange too.

Then they said it.

I can't believe Joanne is no more, and the Wilsons have gone. After the funeral they left – just like that. I thought it rash but grief has no rules. Next thing I knew the house was empty. And now two men have moved in. My husband says they're gay. I've not had a lot to do with them, not yet, though they did poke a Christmas card through the door with an invite to a party. A party? How can we go to a party when Joanne's... no. Definitely not. How inappropriate and they must know about Joanne. Everyone knows. It was in the paper. I don't blame them leaving. It doesn't bear thinking about. We all said we never saw it coming, with her being such a bright girl.

But sometimes I think – maybe we did.

A few months back I started seeing a different young girl in Joanne from the one I got to know and love like a relative. She went around with a boy – there was something about him I never liked. Having nursed children for years I saw something. Our children went to schools out of the area and were driven by their father, so they were not involved with the kids in our area. But still, I should have said something.

I used to see her with the boy and then suddenly she would walk home alone and at first, I was pleased. I know she'd pick up Jimmy from school. The outgoing girl walked with shoulders hunched, pale and avoiding eye contact. "Everything okay?" I asked her once on my return from Mark's corner shop. Evelyn had mentioned they had broken up but she didn't seem to know details. Joanne wouldn't speak about it – which is not like her. I did try. The usual "more apples on the trees for you, my dear, and you are so young to be worrying about boy stuff."

"Hello, Mrs Elizabeth," she replied in an uncertain whisper. That's what she called me *Mrs Elizabeth.* "All good."

But it wasn't, was it? It wasn't all good.

"And that boyfriend of yours?"

"I need to go now, Mrs Elizabeth…"

I suppose I assumed it was what happens, first love then they finish over something trivial but what do you really know about love at fourteen? Just that the bubbly girl we all loved had become a shadow of her former self but it happens, doesn't it and I fully expected a couple of weeks later she'd be over the lad and there'd be another one or she'd be too busy with school. She was always a grade-A student.

But sometimes things don't turn out that way – do they?

She died the day before her 15th birthday.

My neighbour Piper had knocked around lunch time the day it happened, but I had no interest in entertaining her. I was up earlier than usual because, like I said, I was meeting my friend in town who was only about for one day – and had the night shift ahead. Why was the actress even there?

Looking for Joanne it turned out. It seems odd now when I think of it.

There she was standing there – red hair dyed with some golden highlights looking like she'd just got out of bed.

Smelling of fags and whisky. Not that old, in her late thirties maybe but we all know what alcohol does. She was rambling about Joanne, who had called in to see her the day before but she'd sent her away. Piper was a bit incoherent to be honest. Had she been to bed? Was she still drunk from the night before or had she put vodka on her cornflakes? She didn't make a whole lot of sense. She did seem worried though.

I watched her stumble back into the street.

Now I wonder what Joanne had gone to see her about, and I try to talk to her when I see her. She looks like she needs a good wash and her hair, well, in need of shampoo and hair dye, the roots showing through. Not quite the glamorous actress she was. But I feel for her and have even had her in for coffee because I know she must feel the guilt. She doesn't say why Joanne came; she seems to freeze-up when I ask. But I know she thinks if she had spoken to her maybe she wouldn't've—

It's a terrible thing.

Nobody's fault.

We all noticed things. We were all too busy. We all make excuses.

Just as we all carry the burden.

The day after it happened there was a policewoman on my doorstep. A family liaison officer; I recognised her from work. She was talking to all the neighbours about what happened.

The day I came home to the terrible news, to hubby trying not to cry, I'd immediately rushed next door. I didn't think they'd let me in at first. When they did Evelyn was just standing there, like a bewildered animal. I knew that haunted look, I'd seen it too many times in my job and it never gets easier. It was a bright sunny day outside but number 11 felt dark and cold.

That evening my husband cooked a stew and we invited them over. The four of them, including Evelyn's dad – Bert – who was visiting from up north, all slept together in our spare room. Sunday was Joanne's birthday; no one mentioned it. They stayed with us all that day.

After the funeral they said they were leaving, going to their summer place on the coast somewhere. They planned to take everything, rent the house out. I wasn't sure it was the right thing to do, but in grief what is right and wrong? And they'd made up their minds. Evelyn asked me if I could pack up all the things in Joanne's room. It was just too hard. They wouldn't talk about what happened. They had completely shut down. Evelyn did ask me if I came across her diary amongst her things when I packed them – but I have to confess, I never saw it. I looked among all her books; she did love to read and I told Evelyn there was an old beige and yellow book on her bedside table but it must've been what she was reading – because it wasn't a diary. I did poke inside it in case there was a note but there was only a bookmark – near the end. I imagine the police had already looked – picked over her things; like crows at a carcass.

I glance again at the bag, the decorations – so many family memories. The children have taken it so bad, but life has to go on, doesn't it? We can't cancel Christmas even if the Wilsons have. And I'm sure Evelyn will be in touch – when she can, you know.

I come from a long line of strong women. I think about what Gran would have done, and how I owe this life to her bravery. She survived the long lines to exile from her home near the Black Sea.

I watch the pigeons arguing on the fence before I kneel and slowly unzip the big red bag that houses the Christmas tree. Hector watches me and taps me on my knee as he's always done if I look sad; he's an empath.

I can at least set it up in its corner and let the children hang ornaments when they come in. I have them for all my Greek family – memory ornaments and next week I'll pick one out for Joanne. Hang it next to the one for my grandmother. Maybe an angel with blonde hair and blue eyes. The children can help.

The pain is still there; it will always be but no matter what, life must go on.

Carol has an idea we need do more. Do something so it doesn't happen again, only it will, won't it. I'll have a word with her after Christmas. As I wrestle to get the tree free, I catch a glimpse of the way the light dances across the garden and know I am Greek and proud and today need to be strong for my children because they are still here.

As I fix the base and then work upwards bending the branches into shape, I hear my husband's key in the door and my children's voices following him into hallway and for a moment, before we all make a proper start on the Christmas decorations, I will think of the girl with the blue eyes shining like the Mediterranean sky.

The Secret Diary of Joanne Wilson – aged 14 and 5 months, 2½ weeks

To know man is to know his darkness.
                    — J.D. Salinger, The Catcher in the Rye

He wrote my name in small letters inside a heart on the wall. But sometimes I feel as small as the name. I don't deserve him. I'm useless at love. I'm not good enough.

December 31st
Number 12
Piper

When I wake up, it's New Year's Eve.

The sun is low, making triangles across the room. It's then I realise the curtains have forgotten to close themselves. The leather on the sofa has begun to crack and harden from the coldness of the room, leaving my back in pain every morning from my same crumpled-up position through trying to swaddle in some warmth. My arm hangs off the side of the sofa, as if it were a body I was trying to cuddle, my fingers rested in the glass of whisky I fell asleep with. I investigate my whisky-soaked hand and see how it has imbibed liquid into its man-made wrinkles and left a little layer of orange at the bottom of the glass, like mould. *Prawned, again.*

I convince myself it's all there soaked up into my palm like I am a little straw. The light in the room feels white and every time I try to sit up my eyes shut again.

Mist has gathered on the window; I wipe a big gaping circle onto it which makes my sleeve wet. Nothing moves outside except a faint drabble of Christmas lights. The recurring movement of the Santa on the bicycle, all day and night blue lights go round and round. I am sick of it. I can't wait till someone takes them down. The house across the street looms over the square and itself seems to disapprove of the exercising Santa. Before the new people arrived, the house was covered in flowers and candles but the cold made the bouquets die and all the candles were blown out into half-melted pots of wax in the wind. The house turned into its own gravestone. The lights make every morning feel like a repeat of October 13th.

50

Sometimes when I focus on it too much, police sirens get louder in my head and I expect to see a family crying. It only goes away when the curtains are pulled tight together and I get to shut it out.

I lock my door and leave the house, as I have done once every day since October; wearing the same black winter coat. I need a new one, one that doesn't look like a funeral coat. I'm not employed anymore so I have the free time to do whatever I wish. And that means buying whisky from the corner store, from Mark's, where a little bell rings me in.

"Good morning, Miss Marigold. Are you celebrating?"

"Always, Mark"

"You give me enough business for me to be constantly celebrating."

I like Mark. He's funny, and kind to me. On the day the local papers published the story of "Monday and me" he took the papers from the shelf. By the door, Mark has a little basket full of sale items marked with a little red barcode, "on offer". I imagine they are leftovers from Christmas. There's a little fishnet sack of oranges. Monday hated when I ate oranges. He left the room whenever I had one cut up on my dressing-room table.

The sweet aisle is packed full of sugary treats I want to indulge in. When I was a child, I thought I'd buy myself sweets every day because no one could tell me I couldn't. The sweets I could buy myself everyday ended up being alcohol. Now I stand in front of a packet of Tangfastics crying, knowing just how much I let everyone down.

"Just these please."

Mark looks down at the fishnet bag of oranges and Tangfastics that separate us.

"Okay."

Behind him there's rows and rows of different alcohol,

51

next to cigarettes and vapes and everything that shouldn't be sold to a person. Everything that poisons a person.

"Can I have some whisky too, please?"

Mark just looks at me. "I'm hesitant about that, Piper. I'm not sure how well it would go with Tangfastics."

"Quite well I presume, when I find out I'll tell you."

"I think I'd rather not know." He stands with his hands on the desk and the card machine flashes up a price ready for me to pay.

"That's six pounds and twenty-one pence please."

"That's cheap for alcohol." He doesn't find that funny.

"I'm not gonna give it to you, Piper."

I laugh at that. "You're joking?"

"Not today, Piper."

"Not today? Of all days? What if I'm celebrating?"

"I'd love to believe you."

"Oh, right so, so, are you gonna serve *her*?"

An old woman stands behind me. She looks away from us, trying to focus on the ceiling, then the door. I know she's secretly enjoying watching Mark turn me down. She'll probably say something she thinks is funny to him about me when I leave.

"She doesn't buy alcohol from me every day, Piper." He leans forward and tells me through gritted teeth as if to keep some of my dignity. She would have loved to hear that line.

"Fine. Fine then." I sweep my Tangfastics and oranges off the till desk. "If you don't want my business."

"Piper…"

"No, no! It's fine you keep it, selfish twat."

I bet she loved hearing that and the other things I mumble, aimed at her.

When I get home, I rage through the cupboards and find a bottle of champagne at the back and a hidden bottle of whisky.

"HA!" I hold it in the air like it's a trophy. *"Screw you, Mark! Screw. You!"* I didn't need him to sell me anything. I unscrew the cap and throw it across the floor. It burns like acid down my throat. A scorch that feels familiar.

Monday gave me his glass to try at the first cast party we went to. He always drank whisky at parties. I never had it before and I choked on the smell of it and regretted it after. He was playing my husband, Brick, in Tennessee Williams' *Cat on a Hot Tin Roof.* I played Maggie, "The cat". He kissed me after that and told me the taste was wasted on me; he took it back, the empty glass, and crushed his cigarette in it. He introduced me to his wife later that night when she picked him up in a big black car with big blacked-out windows. Her baby bump meant she had to sit a bit further from the steering wheel than she normally would. *"Good job she's tall."* I think that was supposed to be a joke. She was a model, his wife. He was the son of a pop icon in the eighties and he put all his effort into being just as famous. The slightly famous and very adulterous, Monday Parker. And I loved him like he was already mine.

It's getting late and dark and on the television are the random movies they put on when they suspect people aren't watching. One film was about an owner and her dog. *I should get a dog*; everybody seems to have a dog. I nearly finish the bottle. Every time I breathe in or out, I can taste it again and smell it and somehow, he is right here with me.

"Is your name really Piper Marigold?" he asked me when we were staring at the ceiling of my bedroom.

"Yeah." He made me laugh and I loved it when he laughed, how the sides of his smile creased and how real he looked. I'd watch him laugh all day.

"My stage wife, Piper Marigold."
Something about his echoing laughter made me cry.

Above the sofa is our production poster; it hangs high on my wall with Monday at the centre. And when the sun hits him, he looks like a religious artifact. The TV *drolls* on, it hasn't made sense to me for days and I want to leave it, so it can sit and ramble on to no one. A woman speaks on the TV with a smile too wide for her cheeks and she wears a golden dress that keeps making the screen sparkle with little tiny flashes of light. It looks familiar to me, that over-expensive fabric and the way it falls off her shoulders. Monday liked that dress, that's why I remember it, I remember being in it when he zipped up the back and moved my hair over my shoulder, when he told me I was the most beautiful woman, in the most beautiful dress. The most beautiful dress that hangs in a zip lock bag in my wardrobe.

There it is, in all its golden glory. The light still shimmers against it and makes it twinkle like the woman on TV. It hangs over my body now, like a child in her mother's clothes. The hem has dulled and has black marks, and has begun to fray having been dragged against red carpets all night. It's scratchy against my skin; that is about the only thing that feels familiar. We were nominated for an Olivier. I took my mum and my grandmother, who knew nothing about Monday, because I couldn't excuse the humiliation of having to explain why he was kissing his wife on the carpet. I left my family in the lobby waiting whilst I combed through my hair in the mirror trying to breathe and not let my make-up run. I was the most beautiful woman, until we were in a crowded room.

In his acceptance speech he said everything he did, he did for her. I think that must have excluded me. My hair was

54

knotting at the back; my face was splotchy with different patches of red and heavy circles of grey had formed beneath my eyes. Had I become everything he said I was?

October Twelfth

"Actor Monday Parker speaks out against cheating allegations with co-star Philipa Gold", "Parker's wife speaks out about allegations", "Parker rejects cheating claims".

They didn't even get my name right.

My floor felt so cold beneath me but I couldn't manage to move, I couldn't leave the papers and kept moving them over each other, hoping every time the headlines might change. When they didn't, I filled the silence with my screams and cried into the emptiness of my room. Until Monday called.

"Hello, I don't know what's going on."

"What have you done? I don't know why you've done this. This is cruel, Piper. I don't know why you've made all of this up in your head!"

"I haven't, Monday! I haven't made anything up. I didn't tell them, I promise I didn't tell them!"

"I have a family, Piper! This isn't okay! It's not going to get you anywhere!"

"Monday, please, I don't know what's happened, I, I don't know how this got out!"

"Nothing got out, Piper! You've staged this! That's not even me!"

New Year's Eve

"I think Monday might have been a narcissist." That's what I tell my champagne as the cork flies out into the garden. Because he wasn't aware how kissing other women, and sleeping with them in London hotel rooms, might be dangerous when he's married and famous. He cared more about the "being famous" part; if he cared about the "married" part he wouldn't have done it in the first place.

It is ticking closer to midnight and from further away parties get louder and the beat becomes a pulse. I don't enjoy it. The beat is so loud it makes the whole house shake; and when I feel it too much, it becomes the knocking at the door.

October Twelfth

I stayed all morning on the phone to Monday's voicemail, who kept telling me *the person I called was not available.* I could imagine my number on his phone untitled but ringing repeatedly, him telling his wife it was the tabloids.

I knew I hadn't made it up, but somewhere inside I felt this deep betrayal to Monday like, somehow, I was too careless and let it slip from underneath me. When I turned my phone over, I had missed calls from my mum and texts from my friends at the show and a voicemail left by my manager. I had no emails from the tabloids or the press and I realise it's because they spelt my name wrong. I imagined them desperately trying to contact my manager for a statement and nothing showing up. Them frustratingly saying, "NO! I *don't want Piper Marigold*, I want *Philipa Gold!*" They didn't care enough about me to realise they could've had her, had they looked at the programme of the play.

It was three hours before the evening show started and forty minutes before I had to be there for warm-up. When I thought about leaving my house it made my stomach churn. My phone kept ringing with texts and calls from my director. Mentioning Monday not coming in, that he was planning on leaving the show. I ignored them all, the texts were supposed to be a threat to me. *"I've had to call BOTH of your understudies in. You need to tell me if you're coming, Piper."* I seriously wondered if Monday was getting the same treatment or if he was being begged to come in. I wondered if a conversation had been had about *"adjustments that would be made to the play if he wanted to stay."* I spat out my toothpaste and watched it gurgle down the drain and silenced my phone. I was grateful for the silence. I pulled my scarf around my head and wrapped it up around my neck. I was ready to wear my sunglasses in the middle of a dark October to hide my red eyes. A knock at the door made me jump; it was the loudest thing I heard all day. Through the peephole there was the distorted body of a young girl. Joanne. I only ever saw her walking home in her school uniform or walking a dog on a Sunday. I didn't pay any attention to her usually.

"Piper? I'm Joanne."

"I know."

"I, I just wanted to say," she stuttered, "I'm really sorry about what's happening with your play."

"I don't know what you're talking about." Evidently, I did. She knew because the local papers covered it.

"I, I know he's lying. I know it's not true, because I saw him here with you, I saw him in the square." I was prepared to shut the door on her before she revealed that she saw us. Something that was festering inside of me, she, Joanne, had just released on herself.

"You saw?"

She nodded.

Part of me knew she was intending to rile me up, but the humiliation of the day was not about to reinvent itself in the form of a teenage girl telling me what I already knew.

"So, who did you tell? Did someone pay you? Did they give you lots of money? Did you get something out of this? What was it?"

"No! No, I, I didn't tell anyone! I just, I understand, I understand how they've hurt you."

"You understand? You are a child. You cannot understand, this is not a bad day at school, this is not some sort of joke, this is my life. This is my career; I was in love with him! You cannot stand there and tell me you understand because you are a child! You do not understand! You can't! To stand there and tell me you understand is pathetic!" I screamed across the square, lights flashed on in the bedroom window next door, Joanne's cheeks burned red and I saw the embarrassment flood her eyes with tears. "Go away," I hissed. "I hope whatever you got from this is worth it." Joanne blinked and turned to leave. I watched her walk out and shut the gate behind her, as she turned around to look at me watching her leave, her lip quivered and I felt some aching pull in my stomach towards her. Next door a curtain was pulled aside and the old woman looked out. I opened my mouth to call Joanne back but she left and crossed the square, when I shut the door, it made a loud thud.

What I could never have known then was that twenty-four hours later she would be dead.

At the theatre no one spoke to me. I checked for Monday's name on the sign-in page and couldn't find his signature.

"He's not here yet." Paul, the security man, sat in the office flipping over a paper. The first page was noticeably removed, it was the daily papers, I knew because I spent all day looking at them. He was the only person to speak to me. When people passed me in the hallway they pretended to do other things, like flip over pieces of paper or check their headset. I walked into the dressing room I shared with a couple of the extras; they were all sitting there speaking about me. I stood at the doorway, holding the door partly open as they stared at me bug-eyed. Those who just came to talk about the gossip excused themselves and as soon as they were done with their makeup, the girls left too. Not knowing what to say. I was left in the low light of my dressing room, in front of my mirror trying to pin my hair into place. The crying had made my eyeliner smudge and tear tracks were patching through my foundation. I gave up trying and let my hair fall down with just my smudged eyeliner left on.

New Year's Eve
In the living room, the New Year's Eve TV is interviewing families who are celebrating and newly wedded couples, and couples who are to be wedded in the new year. I drink straight from the bottle, feeling instantly sick from the fizzing.

October Twelfth
The opening drums of the play banged through the theatre as I waited by the wooden frame door. I wondered if the sound of the drums bellowed over my beating heart and hid it from the prying eyes; I don't think any sound could have. As the light lifted over the stage, it briefly shone over the audience. Sold out.

New Year's Eve
I can feel the zip of my dress flailing open on my back and it begins to agitate me, the scratchy fabric of the sequins just dangling. Every time I move, the dress falls off my shoulders, and drags in front of my feet. I begin to strongly dislike people who put zips in the back of dresses. I miss how my dress fitted then.

October Twelfth
"Wha'd you say, Maggie? Water was on s' loud I couldn't hearya..." Monday's voice gave me some sense of relief combined with an overwhelming feeling of deep sadness and a new loneliness I hadn't experienced in his presence before.

New Year's Eve
Through the window the exercising Santa spins its blue wheels over and over again. It is so bright it reflects off the frosted-over grass, when I focus too hard, it turns into the police lights.

October Twelfth
I was filled with relief at hearing his sharp southern accent. It wasn't great but people were scared to critique him too much. *"Living with someone you love you can be lonelier-than living entirely alone! If the one y'love doesn't love you."*

The audience's eyes burned into us. It wasn't helping that every line he told me felt like public humiliation. It wasn't helping that he couldn't look at me. It wasn't helping that it was the best performance he'd ever given.

New Year's Eve
The zip agitates me and I become so frustrated I try each way to grab it, and end up circling myself. When I get too dizzy, and I finally, for the last time, give up; Monday's portrait is hanging high on my wall. He was like a God to me; he is like my saviour.

October Twelfth
It felt like he was laughing at me with the audience; what a wonderful role to play. A couple where the woman is so

60

desperately in love with her husband, who wishes to give her nothing.

New Year's Eve
"You look so cool." I swallow a great gulp of whisky from the bottle. "*So cool. So enviably cool!*" I shout in my southern accent to Monday's framed picture, "*So cool, so enviably cool!*" The street light outside casts a reflection on Monday's face, his eyes stare straight ahead, ignoring me. "So enviably, cool."

October Twelfth
"What were you thinking of when you were looking at me like that?"

New Year's Eve
Determined for his attention, I climb my way onto the sofa and stumble in front of his face until our eyes are opposite each other. We are so close, that if he were real, I could reach out and touch his cheek and kiss him.

October Twelfth
"When something is festering in your memory or your imagination, laws of silence don't work, it's just like shutting a door and locking it on a house on fire in hope of forgetting that the house is burning. But not facing a fire doesn't put it out. Silence about a thing just magnifies it."

New Year's Eve
"*WHY I am I so catty?*" I swallow another mouthful of whisky and spit it back out. Drops run down the glass and off the frame, they stain his cheeks as if he were crying. I touch his cheek gently to comfort him. "*'cause I'm consumed with envy, an' eaten up with longing?*" I whisper

back to him.

October Twelfth
"'cause I'm consumed with envy, an' eaten up with longing?"
Monday looked out into the audience and turned to a blonde woman sitting at the front with her legs crossed. His wife. And so I turned to her too.

New Year's Eve
The whisky is sticky and feels damp against my forehead as I rest against him.

October Twelfth
"Y'know what I feel like, Brick? I feel all the time like a cat on a hot tin roof!" I moved from the fake door and walked over to where his body was hunched over sitting on the bed, his fake whisky dwindling between his palms, and knelt down in front of him. I lifted his face so his eyes met mine. He was shocked by this, but leaned forward and practically hissed at me, *"Then jump off the roof, jump off it! Cats can jump off roofs and land on their four feet uninjured!"* For the first time all day he stared straight at me and shouted, "Jump off it!"

New Year's Eve
Wetness forms on my cheeks as salty tears run into my mouth. I am still protecting him, it did not ruin him, it ruined the frame. My frame. My picture. Monday hung it when the posters were first released, he climbed off the sofa and put his arm around my shoulders. "There we are, Miss Marigold, my West End star."

October Twelfth
There were murmured gasps and whispers through the

theatre. What a show. "*I can't see a man but you.*" I did not shout, as I was supposed to, but rested my hand on his cheek.

"*Don't make a fool of yourself,*" he said, through gritted teeth, but this was not Brick, reminding Maggie. This was Monday Parker telling me.

New Year's Eve
"I don't mind makin' a fool of myself over you." I want to embarrass him, humiliate him, but I can't, because the truth is, I will always protect him. When I climb down from this sofa he will hang above me, unmarked and unphased by the whisky splatter. I could rip him to shreds but it will rip me too. My face against his shoulder in all my pin curls, who would it hurt more? Really? He is not spitting whisky at my face on New Year's night.

October Twelfth
I had given him everything I had, I gave him my career, I gave him everything I could and still he needed more. He wanted to hurt me more because he did not want to face the reality of his own selfish actions. "*It made both of us feel a little bit closer to you.*" He sat, unphased at the end of the bed as I rested at his knees. I saw our director hidden by the stage, staring at me, anxiously biting his nails. Flashing his eyes beneath his black eyelashes between me and his wife as if to say "look at her". There was a moment of silence where there shouldn't have been, there was a moment when everybody looked at me. "*You see, you son of a bitch, you asked too much of people, of me, of him, of all the unlucky poor damned sons of bitches that happen to love you!*" My southern accent disappeared and the tears began. I was me, not Maggie. I was talking to Monday again not Brick. The thing about Monday is it would never be enough. His wife was not enough for him,

63

and so he wanted me. I could not be enough for him and so he will want his wife. Nothing will ever be enough. *"And there was a whole pack of them, yes there was a pack of them besides me and Skipper! You asked too much of people that loved you! You, you!"*

New Year's Eve
"...You superior creature. You godlike being," I whisper against his portrait which does not move, does not flinch, does not recluse itself. I rip down the frame and break its wooden corners and smash the glass to the floor and tear through his face and let myself fall to the corner of my sofa. I cannot hurt him. His expression stays the same through all my guilt and hurt and crying and drinking he cannot help; he cannot change anything. He cannot change anything. Because he is nothing but a poster. All I want is for someone to tell me it will be okay.

Monday left after the interval. I was pulled off the stage and our understudies completed the show. All the customers were refunded their tickets if they asked. And I became the girl crying on the tube in her red scarf. People moved away from me and averted their eyes when I looked up as if I was something shameful. My house was cold and empty, and nowhere felt right or comfortable and so I was left tossing and turning and pacing anywhere I could with all the drink I could find. The whisky helped me sleep, filling my senses with nights I felt safe and happy. As much as I hated him at that moment, he simultaneously became the only comfort I had.

The next day, late afternoon, sleeping off the whisky, I woke up to sirens and police cars outside on the square;

people were hovering at their doors, with their mouths clasped. Over the grass a family stood outside the house cradling each other with a young boy pressed against their bodies, and a daughter who was nowhere to be seen.

"What is the victory of a cat on a hot tin roof? I wish I knew... just staying on it I guess, as long as she can... Later tonight I'm going to tell you I love you an' maybe by that time you'll be drunk enough to believe me."

I pull an old white plastic garden chair across the garden and sit in the cold by myself. When fireworks spread across the sky from different neighbourhoods and I hear far off celebrations I know it's twelve and the new year has begun. I lift my glass to the sky and think about Joanne. Maybe we are not so different; she did what she did over a boy. Then I think maybe this year, I'll get a dog.

The Secret Diary of Joanne Wilson – aged 14 years, 6 months, 3 weeks

Unravel the mysteries to find only emptiness
 — **J.D. Salinger, The Catcher in the Rye**

How do you know if he loves you? Am I the only one? I thought love was meant to make you happy? I am losing myself to him. **I need a place where there is no need for me to be perfect.**

January
Number 14
Matt

I'm frozen. I'm standing in the hall, not moving, unwilling even to take off my coat.

The weather is freezing, a damp penetrating cold driven by a biting north wind. No snow though. My mum would have said it was too cold to snow. It's far colder than the cold, dry air of Val d'Isére and there was no shortage of snow there. We got back just yesterday from the luxury skiing holiday we've been on over Christmas and the New Year. We decided to spend my bonus this time instead of putting it into the pension.

I'm back at work tomorrow. If I'm being totally honest, not looking forward to it. Last year was a struggle. The market seems to be moving away from our products and sales are becoming harder. At the same time, sales targets are increasing and sales support reducing. As I said, last year was a struggle. It was only that last-minute completion, quite against expectations, that meant I'd reached my target, exceeded it by a fair bit in fact. It meant a good bonus. But I don't think I can pull that off again. There isn't much in the pipeline and few new areas I can try and tap. Again, if I'm honest, I'm tired of it. I've been in sales for more than twenty-five years. With this company for the last six. They don't pay that well but the bonuses can be spectacular. Trouble is I'm selling, trying to sell, big ticket items. The sort of things that companies don't buy that often. And they take their time over the decision. It means a lot of work, often with no reward at the end of it.

And they're a ruthless bunch. If you're not performing, you're out. I've seen it happen more than once. Being in your late-forties is a dangerous age in the sales business.

Yes, prospects like the experienced man, the product knowledge and the gravitas that age brings. But companies want the thrusting, go-getting of youth. People with few commitments who could work long long days, weeks and months on a deal. I suppose I must have been like that once. I can't remember. Only that it had seemed easier. Despite the eventual good result, last year had been difficult and the year before too, truth be told. I'd only just made target that year. It's been on my mind a lot. The skiing holiday had been a chance to relax and get away from it.

I am so cold because it's my habit to walk to Mark's up the street for the Sunday papers. I suppose having just come back from a ski resort I thought I'd become acclimatised to the cold, not realising how cold it is here in comparison. But it isn't just the weather that's making me feel cold.

I've met two, no three, people from the square – that old woman who lives on the corner was the first and she couldn't wait to tell me about Joanne. We all knew she'd died of course but it seems it wasn't an accident. At least one of them was on the point of asking if I knew anything, seeing that Jack had been her boyfriend.

Jack is my wife's sister's son. They live a few streets away and I suppose he goes to the same school as Joanne. It's Janet's younger sister, Caroline, and she'd married a few years after us. I never took to my brother-in-law. He was charming enough I suppose before they were married, the few times we went out as a foursome. But he always came across as very self-opinionated, and didn't appear to pay much attention to whatever Caroline said. Caroline always appeared to be living a little in his shadow.

After they were married, we'd visit and while Janet chatted with Caroline he and I would go to the pub. He wasn't, he told me, interested in women's talk. But we had little in common. I don't much like football or darts, don't share his opinions and frankly I have enough posturing aggressive men as colleagues, without wanting to share an evening in the pub with one. He seems, to me at least, to be getting worse as he gets older. His views more extreme. *Gays should be locked up away from decent folk. Women being only good for the kitchen and the bedroom. It was important to show them who was the boss.*

After a time, I stopped going with Janet and she now meets Caroline in a café or the park. Janet thinks Caroline has few friends now. Most, it seems, like us, have chosen to stay away. Her husband doesn't make any of her friends welcome.

Janet always returns from these get-togethers a little subdued and sometimes a little angry. She told me that Caroline finds it more difficult to get out of the house to meet her. Her husband wanting to know where she was going, when she would be back, who had she spoken to and what she'd been saying. She had confided to Janet that she knew she'd made a mistake in marrying him. More recently she'd told her that she was increasingly worried about her husband's influence over their son. How Jack was starting to develop the same attitudes and opinions as his father.

I'm warmer now. I take off and hang up my coat. We're planning a late lunch at a local restaurant we both like. Sort of a finale to the holiday before we get back to our everyday lives. So we have a few hours for some tea and the papers. As with all Sunday papers there are heaps of supplements and while Janet settles down with one of the magazines, I take the main paper. But nothing holds my interest and thoughts of Jack and Joanne intrude.

The doorbell had rung one evening a few months ago. End of the summer holidays if I recall right. Janet was out so I was on my own. It was Joanne. I didn't really know the girl despite her living so close. I'm away from home during the day and often working at weekends so I don't know the people in the square very well. I guess I'd seen her around from time to time. She was upset, not crying exactly but I thought she had been. She was clutching her mobile phone and kept glancing down at it, like they all do. She asked if I knew where Jack was. She hadn't been able to get hold of him. I didn't. Wasn't he at home? No he wasn't and he wasn't answering his phone. I suppose I thought it was just one of those teenage love things where her life had been ruined because he wasn't returning her calls and to be honest I had more than enough on my mind without that. I wasn't very sympathetic; didn't ask what the problem was, said something inane like he'll be in touch and not to worry. Something like that and she went away. I went back to my sales plan. By the time Janet came home I'd more or less forgotten about it and I didn't mention it to her.

I don't have much to do with Jack. But, a few weeks later, we'd bumped into one another; one Wednesday I think it was. After the summer holidays. Unusually I was working from home and had popped out for something or other. I thought it was strange that he wasn't at school but remembered that Janet had told me he'd been suspended. I didn't ask him about that. He wasn't likely to talk to me about it. I asked how things were going with Joanne and mentioned that she seemed upset when she'd called round. He didn't look at me, just mumbled something about her being a silly girl, who couldn't take a joke and anyway, they weren't together anymore. Oh well, I thought, teenage love and all that.

I don't much fancy going for that late lunch now. Suddenly, I feel very cold again.

The Secret Diary of Joanne Wilson – aged 14 years, 7 months and 1 day

The true nature of man is the storm within.
        — **J.D. Salinger, The Catcher in the Rye**

I'm not ready, Jack. Please be patient with me...
I'm so lost.

February
Number 13
Edith

Well, that was another close call.

I thought I was going to check out yesterday, pop my clogs or as my Australian friend says "fall off the twig". I know time is running out, turned eighty-two last year, lived longer than most of my friends and family. I need to stick around a bit longer to look after my husband George. We need each other. But it all just breaks my heart as life seems full of loss these days, friends and family, and of course young Joanne last year. I need to get out of here, I'm stuck in hospital again, with my own broken heart.

Yesterday, after getting George outside for his bus to his daycentre, I had a look around the street, waved at a neighbour walking his dog and said good morning. I remember Joanne used to like walking his dog. I look over to her old house; her family moved out soon after her death, and two men are living there now. This time of year, with most of the trees still bare, I can see further across the square. Won't be long before the birch tree will spring to life. Daffodils already seem to be making an effort.

I kept meaning to introduce myself to the new couple but just been too tired or too busy. Most people find it difficult and awkward to meet George now. He doesn't remember what to do either and just looks blankly at me. It breaks my heart to see his abilities and memories fade away.

Sometimes I think about moving into a flat, but we have lived at number 13 for nearly sixty years and it's full of memories. I think it would break my heart to leave it all behind. But then again, thanks to my dodgy heart it will probably be me who dies first. Now I just think I will leave it to the kids – Peter and Sandra – to sort out all our belongings and probably put their dad in a care home. I just feel so gloomy and thinking of death recently, as lost another dear friend, Helen. She used to live just across at number 10 with her four kids and husband Leo. They moved out to Australia, with relatives, hoping for better lives and new opportunities. There's a teacher and her mum living there now.

I miss the happy days we used to have together. Leo used to set up a paddling pool in their garden, let other neighbours' kids in, to cool off on hot summer days. We knew all the neighbours back then, we would gather in the square's garden, or on the street, dads playing football with the kids. Kids in and out of the house, leaving trails of muddy footprints, discarded clothes and toys. There was so much joy and laughter, such happy but noisy days of life on the square. Now it's quiet, gloomy and ever so sad about Joanne's family.

I don't really know much about my neighbours now. Although I heard there's plans to tidy up the communal garden and make it into more of a community space. They will need to clear out the weeds and overgrown shrubs. But be lovely to see the square returned to use. Maybe I could donate the tools and packets of seeds in George's shed.

I have got so many happy memories being in this house, number 13, a lucky number for us. As it was George's birthday yesterday on 13th February, I have been opening his cards for the last week, full of news of how our friends and family are doing.

Sadly, he didn't really take much notice of me reading out the birthday wishes and updates. We used to foster kids and they are now grown up with their families and it's lovely to hear from them. Sadly, some of our foster kids didn't survive long into adulthood, lost to alcohol or drugs.

I sometimes wonder what happened to my next-door neighbour Piper Marigold, local actress. She drinks too much and uses our glass recycling box. I saw it piled up high yesterday morning, when I put a couple of empty jam jars in the box. I hear her late at night putting the bottles in there and think she tries to avoid seeing me during the daytime. I just want to reach out, give her a hug and offer my support. But like many young people, they forget us oldies had young lives too.

I miss John, George's older brother; he was a good friend and my landlord as he bought the house, needing a home for him and his brother. They grew up in children's homes as they lost their parents and siblings during the war. They rented out rooms to help pay the mortgage and bills. I saw the advert for a room and went to see it with my friend Gina. We needed somewhere near the biscuit factory where we worked as secretaries. She stayed for a few years before moving out to live with her new husband. Even when I made more money, I stayed as I loved living there, getting closer to George. He would take me out to dances and to the cinema at weekends. Anyway, poor John, he died young of cancer, in his sixties. He was funny, he and George always playing silly jokes on me and our friends.

John and George set up a coach holiday company, and if I wasn't working, I used to go with them. We used to go all around Europe, seeing amazing places and I would deal with the bookings and tickets, with ill and missing passengers and cleaning the coaches. But mostly I didn't mind, as we visited some amazing places; places we would never have been able to afford ourselves. I loved Venice and on our second trip there, George proposed to me on a boat, it was so romantic except he overbalanced and fell in the canal. He tried again on dry land and cheered when I said, "Yes of course, you clumsy twit."

We had a great life together, tough at times, raising our kids and fostering some troubled teenagers. Both of us wanted to foster kids as we spent time in foster care ourselves. Our families had their troubles, as many did, after the war; older siblings got evacuated and stayed with new families. I was raised by a strong-willed grandmother, who I thought was my mum. Turned out, one of my elder sisters was actually my birth mum. She didn't want me and never liked me. I'm not wasting my time thinking about her. Life is what it is.

We raised our own family with love and care, and I do feel proud of them. Peter, was the first in our family to go to university. He runs his own computer business now. He met Lucy, a primary school teacher, and they have fifteen-year-old twins, Kate and Chloe. I wish I saw more of them but they are always so busy. When I try to talk to them, they just think I am too old to understand their lives. I want to tell them I was a teenager too, with difficulties and challenges but they are always on their phones and they don't listen to my advice.

I check my iPhone to look at photos and recent messages. Peter sorted out the phone and a laptop for me at home, to do video calls with friends and family and shopping online now. Technology helps us all keep in touch. But I like looking though our old photo albums, full of old memories, postcards from abroad. I much prefer a physical card to an email. I wonder what happens when I go. Will our grandkids take an interest in our past lives and history? Will they treasure all the photos and keep in contact with those they shared their home with? It all brings tears to my eyes and I rummage in my bag for a tissue and find my old handkerchief, pretty faded pink with carefully stitched flowers and "mummy" written on it. I remember Sandra took a very long time to make that in school, she wasn't good at craft work or school for that matter. I was always getting phone calls from the school asking where she was. I usually covered for her and said she was poorly, but she often got seen out in the parks or around the shops and ended up doing a lot of detentions. I think it's ironic she works in a school now. But I suppose she is getting paid to be there now!

Her two daughters, Isabel and Rina, not very academic either, but both are in college. Rina is doing hairdressing and Isabel's doing a catering course.

I wonder what Peter will cook his dad. I wonder if Peter got him a card or present; he doesn't usually and I doubt he bought his wife a Valentine's card for tomorrow. I suppose times have changed and people just send digital cards and messages. It was our tradition that I would get the kids to make George birthday cards and I usually bought him a silly one, with cheeky comments inside. Then next day for Valentine's Day, he would buy me a box of chocolates.

So how did I come to be in hospital? Well, I went to the local shops yesterday to get groceries and was debating whether to get him a Valentine's card, but not sure, probably not worth buying any cards, so expensive now and more for my sake than his. He might have made a card at his day centre as he did last Christmas. Reminds me of the kids coming home from school with their creations and me proudly pinning them to the fridge or propping them on the windowsill, except his gifts are given without joy and ceremony. His loss of interest in cards is another loss to bear, and sadly another routine lost to his dementia.

Anyway, where was I? Oh yes, why am I in hospital? Well, there was a young woman looking at the cards, who reminded me so much of Joanne who I'd seen in the shop looking at cards last year. I'd chatted to her about her new boyfriend and school. She seemed so happy to have a boyfriend but then I saw something change in her expression, like she was a bit troubled and unsure about him. I told her it's always tough being a teenager, trying to work out what's best to do. But can offer a listening ear if you need it. She told me she was alright, but thanks for asking. She had asked how George was doing and then she left. I saw her a few times in the spring and summer, going to school or to the shops. She would respond to my greetings but rarely stopping to chat like she used to. It's just so sad and awful what happened to her and the effects on her family.

I knew this year, it couldn't be Joanne, and the young lady was a bit older. The last time I saw Joanne was the day before she died. I'd heard a fuss outside that had drawn me to the window to see Joanne standing outside Piper's; my neighbour's. Not that I have a lot to do with her but I have to say she seemed angry and sent Joanne away. I did tell the police all of this. I hadn't been aware they were acquainted. Anyway, yesterday the shock of the memories of seeing Joanne made me come over all faint and you'll never guess? Well, next minute I'd nearly collapsed on the floor. Fortunately, the young lady came to help me and got me to the chair Mark keeps for us oldies to rest on. She was concerned and phoned for paramedics as I was getting chest pains and feeling breathless. It was lovely as she stayed with me, talked to me about college and her pet cat Scooby, and the mischief he gets into. I knew she was trying to distract me and I thanked her. I said she reminded me of Joanne; she knew of her, same school but was a couple of years older, in sixth form I suppose. She said it reminded everyone of being careful what you post online.

The paramedics were so kind and caring, and took me to hospital. Although it's really boring being in here, as the time passes so slowly, at least having a break, and a rest. I just feel so tired. It's been so difficult looking after George and being unwell myself. I worry about what happens if I go first, as I expect George will end up in a nursing home and I know he will get good care, as he went in one when I had a heart operation two years ago, but it's not the same as me looking after him with all our memories and routines. Then I worry about coping without him.

I miss George, how he used to be, my loving husband, cheeky sod at times but so caring about me, and our family. I hold all my thoughts in my heart and hope he does too. But his dementia just breaks my heart into pieces and I can't put them back together. I know he will always be mine. But I have been losing him bit by bit, not the way Joanne went, all at once, though when I think about that I wonder. I think about the fragility of it all – even our connections to each other.

Sometimes I show George the photographs of us in the garden, in the summer, with the paddling pool and kids messing around with the hose and spraying us and the plants. Or the children pulling silly faces or us going on day trips to the seaside. I would talk about the early days, when we first met and went courting, getting to know each other and falling in love and promising each other we would always look after each other.

For a bit of distraction out of my gloomy thoughts, I talked to the young lady moved to the bed next to me. She is covered in bandages and her leg is in a plaster. She told me she tripped and fell on some ice outside her house. She cheered me up with her humour and we chatted about the joys of being in hospital and I said about George, and my son looking after him. She said she used to look after her mum who had dementia. We shared stories about the daft things they used to do, like her mum wearing multiple blue and white stripey tops at the same time. I said George gets in a muddle putting on clothes in the right order, but got carers in to help him, got too difficult for me to deal with, which is so sad.

It was a very long night, hard to sleep with all the beeping machines, people groaning and snoring. I dozed on and off, and I watched the beautiful sunrise and it was lovely watching the sky changing colours from black to pink to blue and white clouds; it looked like it might snow. My thoughts drifted away, remembering snow ball fights with kids and George, making snow angels in the park. I miss those happy days, always had a busy home, friends and family around us. Never felt so alone as I do now.

This morning, the lady next to me said good morning to me and happy Valentine's Day; her partner had sent her a cheeky digital card and she showed it to me and we had a good laugh about it. I said about what George used to do for Valentines, as one year he got the kids to paint red hearts and left a trail of them around the house. It was so romantic but took ages to pick up all the pieces and wash off the red fingerprints they left everywhere. In the evenings, he put romantic music on and we would dance together around the living room.

After breakfast, a doctor came and did some more heart tests; she told me they will check the results before I can go home. I thought I'm not getting my hopes up. Eventually after a really long day, a few snoozes and chats with other patients, I got the great news that I could go home too, but with the expected bad news that my heart is struggling to work properly, must take more pills and take it easy. The nurse comes and disconnects me from everything and tells me she has spoken to my Sandra, and her daughters are on the way here. I get dressed and packed up and wait and wait and hope I don't get stuck in here for another night.

My granddaughter Isabel arrives in a fluster and says sorry but it took them ages as her sister couldn't find a parking space, so she's stopped on a yellow line. We need to hurry up, she tells me a few times, as she impatiently tries to speed me through the ward. I say a quick goodbye to the other patients and a thank you to the staff.

My stress levels go up significantly being driven home, as Rina is practising for her driving test next week. I doubt she will pass as it's a bit hair-raising as she takes the corners too fast and did some very sudden braking. But I'm grateful to get home, in one piece, just rather shaken. I suggest she might consider a career in speed racing instead of hairdressing!

We go in laughing and find George, Sandra and Peter, watching an old funny film on TV together, and eating takeaway fish and chips. It makes my heart feel whole again and I hope there's some chips saved for me.

The Secret Diary of Joanne Wilson – aged 14 years, 7 months, 2 weeks

Footsteps on paths not chosen leave an unwritten fate.

— J.D. Salinger, The Catcher in the Rye

Will he leave me if I don't do it? I don't know what to do. I can't talk to Mum. Maybe I should talk to Adrian. I can't sleep. I feel sick. I skipped school yesterday.

You are broken.
You are a burden.
You are lazy.
You are a failure.

March
Number 5
Calcutta

The punch isn't low enough to trouble the short-sighted referee.

My torso buckles. I struggle to suppress growing nausea, as my opponent ruthlessly pummels my undefended body. Boos and whistles from the hostile audience drown out all reason. Somewhere in the unrelenting ruckus an insistent bell rings. Too angry to step away, I allow the full force of my right glove to ram into my assailant's throat. Stumbling sideways, I watch my opponent fight for breath before he collapses onto the canvas. I raise a victorious glove and yell at the irate referee to start the count. Strong arms manhandle me towards my corner. Medics climb into the ring barging past me as they rush to treat my opponent.

Blood, pouring from my eyes and nose, decorates my hairless chest. A pungent smell of perspiration fills my nostrils. A wet sponge soaks my face. Calls for a defibrillator stun the crowd into silence. A familiar face works its way to the front of the crowd. Its foaming mouth provides a catalyst.

"He's killed him, that rapist bloody killed him."

Any allegiance I had with the baying crowd, soon evaporates. Missiles are thrown into the ring. A chair narrowly misses my sweat-drenched head and sends the referee reeling onto my opponent's corner post. Fight officials take the brunt of the onslaught. Bouncers drag a section of the audience out of the hall. The face laughs, a glint of light catches my bloodshot eyes. I try to turn away, but nothing stops the knife reaching its target: my exposed neck.

"Take that, you bastard," the face shouts as it charges towards a fire exit.

A young girl with a black dog yells after him, "Coward…"

That's when I wake, or at least partially awake from my recurring nightmare.

Images drift through my confused mind: my dying Maltese mother lies on a hospital bed; a police sergeant, his accusing eyes staring at me as he adds Calcutta Drake to a list of names; in a wheelchair, a prison inmate shakes his fist; my son sobs as he's bundled into a taxi. My mother's lips move but the only sound I hear is ringing; the only smell is from my sweat-soaked sheet and pillow.

The haunting reality of the nightmare hits my solar plexus much worse than any punch.

My brain struggles to banish an endless cacophony of images; my eyes, plagued with conjunctivitis, refuse to open. I reach for my phone; a glass crashes to the floor. The ringing stops, an incoherent voice speaks to the downstairs answerphone.

Mr Tibbs barks his disapproval. A trail of blood follows me into the bathroom.

Dressed in shorts and T-shirt, I carefully slip my plastered wounds into my trainers and open the front door of number 5 Station Square. My black labrador, knowing that his weak spine is no longer up to the task, whimpers his disappointment.

It's seven o'clock on a chilly Friday morning. The pavement and communal garden are buried beneath a dense March mist. I can just make out the edges of the biggest tree, the silver birch.

Dipped headlights struggle to cut through the unrelenting gloom; Dimitri's ice-cream van stutters and coughs its way towards the high street. I jog into the square. The estate agent's sign by Mr and Mrs Wilson's front gate is long gone. New curtains have hung at the windows since December, any pattern or colour, now lost in the gloom. If Mr Tibbs was with me, he'd be giving the house an expectant stare, a hopeful bark, but in either case the result is fated never to change: Joanne will never step through that door again.

My feet smart as I turn into the alley and head towards the park. The recurring nightmare refuses to escape my troubled brain. Joanne's always there, sometimes with Mr Tibbs, sometimes without, but always there, stabbing at my conscience. I question which is worse: the memory of an innocent, young, lost friend or the equally remorseless image of the lifeless boxer dying on the blood-soaked canvas. The answer is profoundly clear: Joanne, every time, no contest. Both killed by me: one through neglect, the other through temper. Both, I should have seen coming. I can't forgive myself for ignoring the warning signals about Joanne, while I was wrapped up in my own stupid life. She never missed an opportunity to walk Mr Tibbs, never tired of talking about her ambitions to see the world, to experience different cultures. I saw less of her in those final weeks, but I expected that. My teenage years were chaotic. Joanne's would have been equally so. I cry into the wind to help support my boy, but with Joanne, I might at least have had a chance. I badger myself to resume the therapy sessions. I suppose, in some minor ways, they did help a little, but they never stemmed the flashbacks; never eased the guilt; never even scratched the surface; so, what's the point?

A prison doctor once told me that some complex memories can take years to subside. I've never considered myself complex, just unlucky – a victim of consequence, always in the wrong place and time. I enter the park and follow the path towards the canal. The more my feet twinge, the wetter my socks become. My pace drops to little more than a jog. Convincing myself that it'll pass I continue towards the tow path. Thick mist envelopes my legs, forcing my feet to turn back towards the park. A morning swim I can do without.

I wonder who phoned; the voice on the answerphone eluded me. It was probably Bill Travis, my trainer, wondering why I skipped the gym yesterday. I still question my decision to climb back into the ring, to convince myself that MMA cage fighting is somehow safer; fewer people die, apparently. Under Bill's guidance, I've tried it twice and won both times, but neither victory made up for the weeks I lost in recovery afterwards. Maybe I am getting too old. If Mum was still with me, she'd be begging me to stop, to find another way to stem my uninhibited aggression, to find something more constructive to do with my hands. But boxing is my life, it makes me feel alive, gives me a buzz. My wife could never understand that, it was one of a whole list of reasons why she ran off with my son. He'd be fourteen now and, if he's anything like me at that age, an adolescent nightmare. I'd be able to help with that. All I need is a call, text, letter, anything. I don't need to know where she is, I just need to know that he's doing okay.

Another runner approaches through the haze. Apparently, her father was Jamaican; I believe he's dead now. Her name's Jada; she's a teacher. She moved into 10 Station Square around six months before Joanne's death.

I nod an acknowledgement. She smiles back. It's 7.45, time for me to head home.

As I re-enter the square, a police patrol vehicle passes and stops outside my house. Two uniforms walk towards my door. Across the road a flash of light at number 3 reveals Abigail's nosy face at a window. I turn back and head towards Mark's corner shop. I need some milk, anyway.

My adult dealings with the police began seven years ago, when I was placed on the sex offenders register for having sex with Cynthia Pickles. Her father owned the face that threw that knife. My fingers instinctively touch the raised scar on my neck. The surgeon told me how lucky I was: the knife had missed my windpipe by two millimetres. Lucky, how? My mum died in the same hospital five minutes before I was admitted. Head-on crash with a drunk driver. She was on her way to pick me up. So, my fault, why is everything always my fault? The wound has healed now, as much as its likely to anyway, but only physically. I'd met Cynthia at an over-twenty-one singles' party. Her age wasn't the only thing she lied about, despite being a month shy of her sixteenth birthday. Her name wasn't Fiona either. My decision to go against the solicitor's advice and accept a police caution, is the worst mistake I've ever made. It cost me my job, as the local school's groundsman, and my few relationships with the neighbours. Unhealthiest of all, it pushed me onto the police radar. Bill sorted me out for a time – time being the operative word. I moved into a caravan he kept in a farmer's field, close to the Essex coast, and ran a county lines drug gang for him. I persuaded myself that it was only a stop gap. Bloody idiot. Initially, it worked out just fine. It gave me a regular income and an, albeit uncomfortable, perverse kind of stability, until... Well, enough said, I got three years; could have been worse; I'd be out in eighteen months. However, for reasons I'd rather not talk about, I put a fellow inmate in a wheelchair for the rest of his short life. Wrong place and time again. I'd served almost four years before being released under licence.

Armed with two pints of milk, I stroll back into the square. The police car's gone. I fill Mr Tibbs' food and water bowls, sweep away the broken glass from the bedroom carpet, shower and redress my wounds. Pulling on a jumper and jeans, I press the answerphone and listen to the police requesting me to go to the station, but first – breakfast.

The last time I was shown into this interview room, I was five months younger. It's had a much-needed coat of paint; shame they didn't take the opportunity to change the drab grey colour on the walls. There are four chairs, one table and one tape recorder. I'm told to sit and wait. I remain standing. Just as on my last visit, the fluorescent above my head, still doing its bit to protect the mayor's budget, flickers. The wall sockets and switches are still pissed. I notice stuff like that – get it from my dad, bless him, he was an electrician, fell down a lift shaft. He was thirty-six; I was ten. No one has ever died naturally in my family.

A familiar face steps through the door. He's in plain clothes, middle-aged, bald, lived-in face. The face of a fighter, like mine but with fewer scars. He places a folder on the desk, pulls out a chair, flashes his warrant card. His fingers hover over the record button, but fall short of switching the machine on.

"DI Coalman. This shouldn't take long. Just a couple of questions. Take a seat." I wonder why he feels the need to re-introduce himself.

"I'm okay standing. Should I call my solicitor?"

"That's your prerogative. I only have a few short questions. No-one's accusing you of anything."

I shrug. "Okay, let's get this over. I've places to be."

"Fair enough, feel free to leave whenever you want." His voice matter of fact. "Where were you at midnight last night?"

89

"At home, probably asleep. I went up around eleven; read for a bit first. What's this about?"

"Can anyone confirm that?"

"No."

"You work the door at Johnny's Club, don't you? But you didn't go last night. Why was that?"

"How I run my life is no concern of yours. What's this about?"

"The sooner you stop with the attitude, Mr Drake, the sooner you can mosey back into your sad life. When were you last there?"

"At Johnny's? That would have been Wednesday night, finished around 1.00, 1.15."

"Any trouble?"

"Fairly quiet. There was a singer planned, but she didn't show. Her loss."

"Are you acquainted with a Mr Bill Travis?"

"I know him, why?"

"He was shot and killed last night. When did you last see him?"

Unable to hide the shock, I pull out a chair and fall into it.

"Joanne Wilson." His sudden change of tack takes me by surprise. "I've been reading through my notes; you stated that you'd last seen Joanne arguing with a lad in Station Square. Do you remember what they were arguing about?"

He obviously never believed me the first time.

I pointed to the file. "You've read my statement. I've nothing more to add."

I return to my feet and step back to the door.

"As I said, Mr Drake, you're free to leave whenever you like. However, before you do, did you see them? I trust you look at social media?"

"Them?"

"I'm sure you know what was on social media?"

"No. Like I told you before."

"But the day of the argument… remind me what was said."

Seems he's not giving up, so best to oblige.

"The one thing I do remember was Joanne's angry tone. I'd never heard her raise her voice before, even when my dog growled at her for not letting him chase one of the neighbour's cats. My left ear was bandaged so I couldn't make out what they were arguing about. The only word I do remember hearing was 'post'. When I approached them and asked Joanne if everything was okay, the boy scarpered. Joanne just nodded and ran off towards her home. I never saw her again. When I heard the news, I was mortified, the whole square was, and still is."

"Was he bullying Joanne? Do you think he encouraged her in any way to do what she did?"

"I told you. I didn't hear him, but if he did—" I could feel the anger.

"When did you last see Mr Travis?"

He's wise to change subject though the man's like a bloody yo-yo.

"A few days ago, at the gym."

"You knew him quite well, didn't you? Did he have any enemies?"

"He used to be my trainer."

"It'll save us a lot of time, if you stick to answering my questions. He lived in your place while you were banged up, didn't he?"

"You obviously know that, so why are you… Look, I wasn't his keeper. As far as I know, everyone at the gym seemed to like him. Whoever else he associated with is beyond me."

I turn back to the door. "Now if that's all, I've got a busy day."

"Mr Tibbs," the man pauses, he's waiting for a reaction, "have you ever heard of anyone calling themselves that?"

"What are you talking about?"

"It's a name on Joanne's phone. Have you ever called yourself that, Mr Drake?"

"If you've read my previous statement, you should be aware that Joanne and I knew each other quite well. She loved my dog and up until just before she died, walked him whenever she could. True not as much as she did before but she had a soft spot for him. Mr Tibbs is my dog's name; it's what we used whenever she asked if it was okay to walk him. If I texted back 'Mr Tibbs says yes', I would take my dog to her door. Like I said, if, you read that file, you'd know all about that, wouldn't you? So, unless you tell me exactly what it is you're fishing for, I'll be on my way."

"Did Joanne ever confide in you, Mr Drake?"

"What are you implying?"

"Have you got her diary?"

"Diary, why would she give me her diary? As I've already told you, no. Have you asked the boy at number 8 Station Square? I often saw her talking to him. I assume you have questioned him?"

"Remind me, Mr Drake. Why you were put on the register?"

"That was six years ago. Why don't you lot give it a rest?"

"We never, ever forget, Mr Drake. Not ever. You'll do well to remember that…"

I want to say again how I am only on the register because of a stupid underage girl who lied but I keep my mouth shut. I bunch my fists. I'd never wittingly kill a soul but that boy who…

The slamming door reverberates through the building.

92

The Secret Diary of Joanne Wilson – aged 14 years, 8 months and 2 weeks

I'm the doctor, and I save people
                                    — **The Doctor in *Dr Who*, BBC**

The headaches are getting worse. I can't walk Mr Tibbs again this week. I went to see the doctor today. Mum's phone rang – she's always on it for work so I said I'd go in on my own. I prefer it that way. He gave me a prescription. I told Mum it was for my period pains. She'll never understand. The doctor said it's normal at my age – too much screen time, exam stress. **I'm so hopeless.**

April
Number 8
Adrian

I'm standing looking out from the living room window; my thoughts as low and miserable as the dull April weather.

I had planned to go into town; it's what I usually do on my day off. No lectures today. But since it happened, I don't feel up to it.

From here I can see number 11, just a few doors down from ours. There are catkins on the silver birch in the communal garden opposite. It's something I'd never notice, let alone make a comment about, but I remember last year, something Joanne said. She said the male catkins, which are yellow and hang like lambs' tails, are actually the ones that release pollen to fertilise the female catkins on the same tree. She said the male ones always stand out more than the female. She said it's the same with birds, often the male is the brightest. But that's not always true – is it?

She was so bright. Better than me. Way better than *him.* She wanted to go to uni, study English lit.

Joanne always shone the brightest… until she didn't.

My reverie is momentarily interrupted as I watch a trickle of rainwater wind its way down to the bottom of the window. Then me mum comes and stands beside me as if reading my thoughts. "I can't believe it's been almost six months," she utters. "It was an awful thing that happened." She turns to me.

It's what everyone talked about for months though even that is stopping now, maybe out loud but you can't stop what's inside your head, can you? They still think it. I don't answer. Me dad is sitting in his favourite chair pretending not to hear, reading the local paper. I see him put it down and now he looks from Mum to me. "I was talking to Elizabeth next door," he says, "and she thinks that Carol is thinking of starting a campaign to get some kind of memorial for Joanne."

"Sounds like a good idea," Mum says, "and any publicity would keep it in people's minds and it might stop such a terrible thing happening to someone else."

Isn't it always in our minds? In mine it is.

But then I think – maybe she's right. If people stop talking about it, it's like she was never here. But she was here. She…

Dad nods in agreement. "Carol obviously hasn't started anything yet, but I think the plan is to do something later in the year. You know, for the anniversary maybe?"

"They should do something in the communal garden, so everyone can be part of it," Mum says.

"Yeah," I whisper. Though it needs a bit of a tidy up. I don't say that part.

There's silence for a moment as we sink into our separate thoughts.

"The question is why," says Mum, "I've heard rumours. Too many rumours. Not that I saw whatever it was they said made her do it, but surely a bright girl like that wouldn't do something so silly all because of a boy. Had to be more to it. Elizabeth hasn't heard from the family but she did say Evelyn surely must've realised something was wrong. She said there's been a rise in depression in teenagers. And she said she had seen Joanne and her mum going into the surgery on the square. Do you suppose it had anything to do with the depression? She must've been depressed if she did what she did." Mum turns back to the window and busies herself tidying a vase of daffodils she picked from the garden this morning. "Such a waste of a young life," she adds in almost a whisper.

I can see that Mum's gaze, like mine, has settled on number 11 and being a mum, she's not stopped thinking about Joanne's family. Her mum and dad, brother Jimmy and grandad, Bert, moved out after the funeral and Simon and Schu live there now. No one has really got to know them, although not long after they moved in, they did invite us all to a Christmas party. No one went. I mean, we all thought it was inappropriate. Maybe they didn't know about Joanne. Surely someone must've told them by now.

I sense Mum and Dad's stares and wonder if they're thinking about the same thing. I hear Dad's sigh. Then I hear Mum say, "She was such a pretty little thing too, and only fourteen..."

"Fifteen!" I say.

"That's right, it happened the day before her birthday."

Another silence fills the room before Mum says quietly, "I know you don't like talking about it, but me and your dad get the feeling you two might have been *more* – like you might have been *her boyfriend*. After she broke up with that other boy, that is."

"Mum!" I glare at her. "I wasn't her boyfriend. She was too young for me. I barely knew her!" The last part wasn't quite true.

"Only by a couple of years. That's nothing."

I give Mum a sideways glance. She's right of course. And I always liked Joanne, more than I ever let on. Part of me thinks, though I never say it out loud, that if she hadn't died, we might have... you know... got together. Eventually. I did tell Lucinda that.

"We liked to talk," I say, realising Mum and Dad are waiting for an answer. "Because I suppose I... I felt sorry for her." There. I'd said it.

"Sorry for her? Did you know she was depressed then?" Mum quickly adds, "I thought you said you barely knew her."

96

I'm feeling uncomfortable now, about the direction the conversation seems to be heading. "Look, you know we went to the same school, and lived so close, well I happened to walk home behind her one day and I heard her crying. So I asked her if she was okay and after that, I guess we became like friends."

Mum and Dad look interested now.

"So," Mum says. "Did she say how she was really feeling? Did you know she—"

"No, I had no ideas he was going to... look, I felt sorry for her and we'd talk. I just think she needed someone to vent to, that's all. And once she knew she could trust me, it all kind of flooded out."

Like it seems to be doing now. I've been holding it in for too long. So, as I find myself circling the room, I avert my gaze and pull my seat to face the window and sit across from them.

"Jack," I begin, "the boy."

Mum and Dad look at one another.

"Well, he wanted more than she was prepared to give." Mum and Dad can guess where this is going and they look as uncomfortable as I feel.

"Go on," Mum says.

"Well, Joanne said he wasn't as nice in the end as she thought and he put a lot of pressure on her to get her to *do things*." *God, how do I even put this?* "Things she wasn't ready for. Things she didn't want to do."

"Things?" Dad says. *Like he doesn't know what I mean?*

"Sexual things," I say.

"And did she?" he says.

I shake my head. "He put a lot of pressure on her but she said that as much as he coerced her, she never went as far as he wanted."

"Far enough though?" says Mum.

97

"Poor kid!" Dad says.

"He has a lot to answer for," I say. "The bastard." I add quickly, "Sorry, Mum. But where was his respect, eh?"

Mum dismisses it with a quick gesture of the hand. "I can think of a few worse things to call him." She proffers a wry smile. "She was a lucky girl to have you to confide in. There can be a lot of peer pressure on kids today and from what you say, Joanne did a lot to stand up to that boy."

"Yeah, and look where it got her." I could feel the heat rising in my cheeks. "I just wish I could have done something. I realise now how important it is to have someone to talk to, but I know I should have asked her a lot more, got her to tell me more."

"Now, don't you blame yourself, Adrian. Every one of us will have thought that, but you did more than most. You cannot be held responsible for what she did. And I know who I blame. If she had been your boyfriend, I know you would never have treated her like that and maybe—"

"She'd still be alive?" Dad says.

I shake my head. "I don't blame myself." I rise from my seat. "I'm going to my room. I've got college stuff to do."

"That can wait!" Mum says. "There's something we want to talk to you about." Her eyes shift to Dad who nods. "It's something we've wanted to ask you for a while. And now we seem to be talking about this, *finally...*"

I sit back down and look from one to the other. "What?"

Dad takes in a deep breath. "Well, when all of this was being investigated and the police asked lots of questions, it came up, well actually her mum and dad said Joanne always kept a diary and the key, they seem to think, was on her when... she was found. But they were never able to find the diary itself."

"Yeah, I believe so," I whisper.

Mum and Dad are staring at me intently now. *What do I say?*

98

"Leading up to her death," Dad says, "her parents knew she was stressed but put it down to breaking up with the boy and exam worries, starting her final year… you know. Usual teenage things. They said they never saw it coming. Had no idea she would… They never found the diary."

"Really?" I feign surprise.

"But if they could find it, they'd maybe get to understand."

I don't respond.

"Your mum and me, think she must have entrusted someone close to her to maybe keep the diary safe for her, in case they searched for it."

"I suppose so," I say.

"And you may remember before they left, her parents appealed to friends and neighbours, to anyone who might have it. But no one came forward. It was no doubt locked, but they had the key. So my guess," she now looks at Dad for support, "*our* guess is whoever she gave it to, she made them promise to not let anyone know. But given what's happened, we think they ought to come forward now. Her mum and dad have a right to know what was happening in those last few months of her life. Me and your dad have kept quiet about this, but now you tell us you were close, she confided in you and well, you can see where this is going. If there's something… *anything*… you know or have, any information… they need to know it."

They're right of course.

"Me and your dad have kept quiet but we've often wondered. I remember that just before she died, I saw you talking to her out by her front gate and I know you went into her house…"

"Why was that?" Dad says.

Now it's my turn to take a deep breath. Seems like this is really happening then…

"I don't like keeping secrets."

"And you shouldn't have to," Dad says.

I lean close to the window and stare out at the April showers. I feel Mum and Dad staring at me, watching me closely but they are at least now leaving me to my thoughts.

Since Joanne's diary contains her thoughts and maybe what lead her to do what she did, it has been on my mind constantly since her death. It's obvious everyone, especially her parents, must have been desperate to know more. Was it what that boy did or had this been something more? How long had she felt that way? I suspect the answers are in there. If the family hadn't moved away as quickly as they did to their other house, then I might have seen more of them and maybe, maybe we could have spoken and... too many ifs, you can't build a life on that though, can you.

I turn back to Mum and Dad and Mum reaches out, grips my arm. "Tell us," she says, "when you went into Joanne's house that day, she gave you something, didn't she."

It's more a statement than a question.

I look them both in the eye and nod.

"Yes," I say. "She gave me her diary."

The Secret Diary of Joanne Wilson – aged 14 years and 9 months exactly

The universe houses a tapestry woven from unanswerable questions.
> — **J.D. Salinger, The Catcher in the Rye**

6-month anniversary – Jack wanted me to show him my boobs! I let him feel them but I made him stop. I hope he doesn't break up with me ☹ Would he do that if he loves me?

I'm a quitter, a failure, and a coward

May
Number 2
Danny

I've always been invisible. It could be a superpower but it's not.

I'm nondescript, a blender, somebody nobody notices, just the way I like it. Couldn't do what I do if I had bright ginger hair, weighed 300 pounds and stood six foot tall. I could read scores of books about positive life choices and actions that insecure people lap up, but none of them had a Big Louie to guide them. The memory of my short stay at Her Majesty's pleasure changed my life.

"Accept the fact you're a first-class burglar, Danny. Just cos you got grassed on don't change that."

"I'm still here though."

"Circumstances beyond your control," said the big man. "When you get out, find yourself a proper job, nothing fancy, it keeps them off your back. You pay taxes and become a ghost. Then you can do what you do best. You're not the first inmate I've given that advice to."

I always think back to that conversation. Louie, the motivational speaker for the criminal classes.

I managed to acquire my employment as a postman through a short-lived government scheme for the rehabilitation of young offenders overseen by my parole officer. I fully embraced Big Louie's guidance. That was ten years ago. Even now when I'm pounding the pavement during the day I can't resist being on the lookout for opportune moments.

I was delivering post to a row of upstairs flats above a small parade of shops when I noticed a man in a sharp suit exit the rear of a betting office. I was behind a dumpster bin and observed him place his briefcase on the floor and turn away to answer his phone. I snatched up the case, placing

102

it inside my large red hand truck. I quickly went through an alley onto the high street and briskly moved further along. I watched as the man ran out onto the street clearly in a panic. I thought I was in the clear.

The case contained a brand-new laptop, several memory sticks, documents in a foreign language and £1000 in £50 notes. I took one of the notes and decided on a trip to the pub. I slid the briefcase under my bed.

Saturday evening meant my regular trip to the Castle pub with the usual crowd. I playfully flirted with Beryl the barmaid until her boyfriend Jackie arrived. He was soon into his jokes, mostly politically incorrect but nobody cared. They were a good crowd and left me feeling happy. My mood was tempered by the thought that I would have to leave early the next morning to visit my mum.

I'd never known my father, developing a very close bond with my mother. She'd always been capable and strong mentally out of necessity. I'm not sure if any of those traits were passed on but I could always confide in her.

I was feeling a little cocky, thinking I'd escaped detection regarding the stolen briefcase, but my world was suddenly going to change. Several days later, a different man turned up at my home with a muscular colleague. They knew everything about me, threatened to harm my mum and generally terrorised me.

"You can keep the money; I'm only interested in the briefcase. I hope you haven't done anything with it."

I knew there was no point in lying, the man's companion was obviously used to violence.

"It's under the bed." I retrieved it for him.

"Thank you. I've managed to compile quite an interesting file about you, Daniel. I have a proposition for you. Realistically you don't have a lot of choice, but I'll spell it out for you anyway. You're going to be working exclusively for me until I decide otherwise."

"What about my postman job?"

"It's in everybody's interest for you to continue with that. Just refrain from this other petty nonsense. It would displease me."

He proceeded to tell me what he wanted. Now I'm forced to undertake specific projects. I break into laboratories, security-guarded facilities, stealing and photographing anything my employer requires for his secret needs. I've no idea who he really is and don't want to know. I'm forced to live my life in some type of modern-day servitude. I do the work, get paid and don't inquire.

It's given me the opportunity to put Mum into a private care facility instead of an awful council run one. She has a large room to herself with doors to a manicured garden, expert medical care and expensive drugs to improve and stave off her dementia. Now, for periods of my visits she recognises me. The first time after countless months she called me Daniel. I cried.

My mother bought number 2 when Mrs Thatcher was selling off everything including council houses. My name was put on the deeds.

"Always be a safe place here for you," she said.

I would never be able to afford the house in this street today.

Despite the subtle threatening backdrop continually present, I've settled into a surprisingly comfortable way of life. It's precarious, overseen, but nonetheless satisfying and even exciting at times. I have friends from the daytime and money from the night. In a weird way it's enhanced my life, making it more materialistic which has surprised me as it's never been my vision. I've been thinking more about relationships and the future, grown-up stuff, all rather daunting and overwhelming. Obviously, I'm also permanently aware how it could all come crashing down at any moment.

What with prison and keeping a low profile, I've avoided being involved in the cavalcade of events and people's problems like other residents. Everybody seems aware of each other's lives to some degree which made me more determined to stay aloof.

The terrible incident all those months ago has created a powerful unsettling undercurrent. I'm pleased Mum wasn't around to witness what went on. I'm not aware if she was involved with any of the people caught up in the tragedy. She used to be the focal point for any human stray needing a cup of tea and motherly advice, so it's quite possible. I always remember the times I would see her chatting to locals walking their dogs, sharing brief comments with passing schoolchildren or handing over some of her baking successes. She brightened people's lives with her empathy and positivity. It's so sad to witness her life now.

Since the tragedy involving that young girl, it seems that neighbours have been in contact much more. Residents stop for a chat; there appears to be a coming together to share what happened and reflect. In some way I could feel slightly guilty that none of the past events have really affected me. It's obviously been traumatic for people around here. I'm constantly witnessing comments and attitudes all sprinkled with negativity and sadness.

Obviously other families were more involved in various ways than I ever was. I've been caught up in this and I've gradually started to become visible. People make a point of talking to me and expecting a point of view. It's been a strange experience and I'm starting to feel part of the community in a small way.

This gradual inclusion into a fuller life has coincided with me becoming closer to Ruby who works at the depot in the office. She's funny, pretty and seems to like my company. She has a six-year-old son from a one-night stand with an Australian guy who'd moved back home unaware he was a father.

"I was drunk, he was a loser. It's best this way," she said.

The three of us spent May Day together. We went to a local park with swings and a boating lake. Her little boy didn't speak much but gripped my hand tightly as we walked around, continually looking up at me. I found us a table in the shade at the café. I waited until we'd finished our lunch before mentioning an idea that was on my mind.

"There's something I wanted to talk to you about," I said. "I know all the aggro you've been getting from your creepy landlord, so I was thinking, what about you and Sam moving in with me. There's loads of room and Sam can have his own bedroom. What do you reckon?"

Ruby suddenly became emotional. "That would be amazing."

Sam moved next to his mum. "Are we going to be a proper family?"

"Yes, Sam," I said, looking at them both. "A proper family."

Obviously, she doesn't know about my nocturnal pursuits, so I'll have that problem to deal with in the future if everything carries on with us being more permanently together. She had no issues with my old history so I'm hoping that the shadier aspects of my life won't drive her away. Knowing Ruby as I think I do, I'm not envisaging any problem.

I walk up the steps of my house with our own post. Apart from Ruby's *Puzzler* magazine, most of it's destined for the

106

recycling bin. I've had this route since Christmas. It's been interesting and somewhat enlightening seeing the correspondence I push through my neighbour's letter boxes. It emphasises what a mix of characters live here. I imagine that most streets in Britain are the same.

All of May's periodicals are in my sack ready for delivery. *Amateur Gardening* and seed catalogues at number 3. *Mystic World* and *Tarot Monthly* for number 4 and at number 10 *The Educator*. *Modern Lifestyles* and *The Stage* through the door of number 12 and a couple of Oldie magazines to others. There's also the *Lancet* for number 7, the surgery.

I don't think the doctor is well liked. People seem to think that he should have helped the young girl who died more than he did. Apparently, he was aware of her problems and did nothing. I know my mum thought he was okay, always ready for a chat, so, I'm not sure what to think.

So, as you can see, all my neighbours have their own glossy life choices to embrace. Sometimes there are nondescript plain brown envelopes and packages for siblings and family members. I always wonder what's inside.

As I know too well, everybody has secrets.

The Secret Diary of Joanne Wilson – aged 14 years, 9 months and 3 weeks

That's the whole trouble. When you're feeling very depressed, you can't even think.
— J.D. Salinger, The Catcher in the Rye

I can barely write. I'm crying too much. I am so worthless.

June
Number 6
Carol

Destiny beckons.

Who would have thought that me, Carol Sargeant, a reserved widow, should feel so deeply to be able to overcome my reluctance and get involved. Nevertheless, in the light of recent sad events, I gladly accept my duty. I want to stand up, be counted and join the fight to improve women's overall safety, especially as this campaign is directed against bullying and abuse. The "destiny" word came, as it's said "out of the mouth of babes" and young Joanne was little more than a babe herself when she uttered that short saying. Now it does indeed seem to be my destiny.

Earlier last summer, while out dog walking and having met Joanne, I related my participation in a vigil and group march in central London. It ended at the Houses of Parliament. This was held in an attempt to badger the government's improvement of women's safety laws. The catalyst for the march had been the kidnapping and killing of a young woman, literally snatched from the London streets. I totally agree with the group's other campaign too. It's an online safety bill aimed at making sure this child protection bill, does not get watered down. Joanne must have picked up on my commitment to this movement to make her utter the destiny idea. Of course, I failed to reveal another more personal reason to get involved. In my earlier years my first husband had driven me to a point of contemplating suicide when I too was a coercive control victim. Even though this situation is in the past, I remain unprotected from feelings of depression and anxiety when learning of others suffering similar experiences.

Oh dear! I must stop these bad thoughts; employ the therapy I was taught by doing something pleasing to help encourage a positive attitude. I know, I'll do some baking. I've been meaning to try that lemon drizzle cake recipe taken from a magazine last week. On second thoughts, I will make two, and take one for Sue when we meet this afternoon. Before I can begin, I must pop along to Mark's corner shop; I need some lemons! My little dachshund "Sausage" looked up hopefully from his bed, oops! I had been talking my ideas out loud! He had interpreted it as walk time, no change there, he wagged his little tail expectantly.

Would you believe it! Upon my return from Mark's shop I met Piper, the actress lady from number 12.

I was quite taken by surprise when she began talking.

"Hello!" she shouted as she walked across the street towards me. "I would like a word to apologise for my appalling behaviour when we last met at Mark's shop."

"Think nothing of it," I replied. "I had forgotten, all water under the bridge now." But she was determined to carry on. "I want to tell you how I am a changed person, no more outbursts. I have got myself a pet dog. He is so sweet. I adore him, and being responsible for his welfare is keeping me on the straight and narrow. I guess you can call me a recovering heavy drinker."

"Oh," I replied, "that's really good news, may you continue to be successful."

I sincerely meant that as my mind strayed to that embarrassing encounter a few months ago when Piper, quite tipsy, was verbally abusing poor Mark. He was just trying to dissuade her from buying further supplies. "And what are you looking at?" She rounded on me who was innocently waiting to be served. She called me a nosy parker and added a few expletives for good measure. Anyway, it's a very difficult path she is trying to tread so good luck to her.

Even when baking, my thoughts can't help straying; poor Joanne, it's now about eight months since she took her own life. It is so sad. At first there seemed a dearth of facts surrounding this tragic event which created much speculation among the residents of Station Square. Understandably her parents remained unforthcoming. They no doubt shoulder some blame for not realising the enormity of their daughter's situation. It all started it seems with a simple but likely naive action by Joanne, but no one could have anticipated the outcome. Since young people like Joanne are on their phones so much, it makes me wonder if all those sites discussing and championing suicide might have encouraged Joanne in some way. Because of this, sanctuaries are so desperately needed to support people plunged into unmanageable situations. What more reason could one need to take up this challenge and try to make a difference.

On contemplating the events leading to Joanne's demise I cannot overcome the awful feeling of being like the unhelpful character in the Good Samaritan parable. If only I had intervened, could it have altered things? Though I do wonder about the doctor who lives next door because I had noticed Joanne visit a number of times last summer. She always seemed to be with her mother, mind But I am not one to speculate. I have since heard rumours that the doctor ought to have done more to help, but you could say that of all of us. I've hardly seen the doctor since and his wife barely looks me in the eye. I have a feeling the surgery will close permanently if it isn't already as they never seem to be open these days.

It does not do to place blame on things we don't know.

I think all of us have shouldered some of that but we cannot blame any one person. Unless... well, we all know what her boyfriend did. I prefer not to dwell on that. I still believe we all had an obligation to do more.

Although Joanne and I chatted reasonably while out dog walking and allowing our pets their own social interactions, we really had little in common. I was aware of how kind and helpful a character she was; even her dog-walking was aiding a neighbour. Admittedly I was somewhat aware of changes in Joanne's personality. Going, as she did, from a happy quiet but confident girl, attending school with a group of friends, then having a boyfriend in tow who accompanied her on her dog walking expeditions. Sadly, this precluded any interaction on my part. Then, later I witnessed a different Joanne. She went to school on her own, or with previously unknown bad company. The boyfriend had disappeared. She continued to exercise her neighbour's pet, but even that seemed more sporadic. When she did, she always managed to avoid any of my attempts to chat. It didn't feel good. Unfortunately, I took it personally.

Nevertheless, my little doggy companion was and remains a godsend. People seem attracted to my Sausage. He is so lively and friendly and seems to encourage people to pet him; consequently they talk to me. I too encourage these contacts being a widow of many years and in her seventieth decade, it has certainly been instrumental in my becoming involved with the maintenance of the communal garden in the square. I have become quite good friends with Abigail who lives at number 3. I have donated much time along with many plants and in return have had the pleasure of seeing them flourish while happily enjoying the company of several other neighbours. It's such a win-win. However, I must cease this introspection – my baking has

113

been a complete success – it is a beautiful sunny afternoon, I have arranged to meet my friend, Sue, who lives a few streets away. It's been some time since we last met so Sausage and I have agreed to call on her. I am sure I will enjoy her uplifting company, I need a break from sad reflections. I feel certain she will be pleased with my lemon drizzle cake. It has been quite a success. I will update her with the results of my new campaigning actions, joining the vigil, marching in London, and regale her with my new plans for setting up local help for victims of abuse. She is definitely going to be surprised. I wonder whether she would be interested in joining.

Undoubtedly, she will also be totally amused when I finally report my tea leaves reading experience with Maisie Patterson. Although this lady is a neighbour, the reading was Sue's idea. I only agreed for a bit of fun but it turned out anything but. Maisie certainly takes her "gift" as she calls it very seriously indeed and all those dolls she has placed around the room, fascinating but truly creepy. So many eyes – all focussed on yourself like they're taking everything in. It made the hair on the back of my neck stand on end. In the cold light of day, I did wonder whether, as a child, Maisie had been toy deprived. She certainly hoards; I have never seen so many things! Anyway, it turns out the tea leaves did know a thing or two! They related my ideal childhood followed by my much suffering as a young adult. You could say that again! What's more they knew I had been twice married with both partners having passed over. Well, I am still sad at losing my Ben and guess I always will be, but as for my tormentor of a first husband, good riddance, I couldn't receive better news. Nevertheless, apart from that last detail I was well aware of my past life. It's the future, the unknown, that's of interest. With no messages from Ben, (Maisie was quick to assure me they didn't always "come through"). However, she seemed to already know of my unadvertised idea of selling up home and moving to the coast down south; she disappointingly said a project involvement would put changing my location on the back burner for the foreseeable future. I was sceptical, hence my delay in acquainting Sue with the outcome. Any idea of leading a project was well outside my comfort zone and I said so. Maisie then took on an inscrutable attitude, sort of smiled mystically, mentioned something of one's destiny (that word again)! Then just said, "We'll see."

As expected, Sue was delighted with my cake gift exclaiming, "Oh how lovely, lemon drizzle – my favourite!" She also appeared very interested in my news. I certainly enjoyed the big smile which crossed her face in response to the "no moving" report and happily encouraged me to accept the funny side regarding Maisie's dolls by laughing out loud. However, a more serious attitude overcame her as I outlined my national and local campaigning ideas. Sue admitted surprise at my commitment but readily offered her company on any future vigils or marches. She also agreed to help in any way with the organisation of the memorial proposed for the first anniversary of Joanne's passing. I said, "I am hoping this service will become a catalyst for the setting up of a local victims' support group. Sue then told me that she had been researching youth self-harm and suicides since Joanne had brought the situation so close to home. Do you know, suicide rates for fifteen- to nineteen-year-olds are the highest they have been in thirty years. It is a shocking picture of young peoples' mental health in this country."

I totally agreed, something must be done. They need proper government support programmes in places like universities and schools. It's the only way suicide rates can be reduced. Campaigns must push for government funding especially where people struggle to get the support they so desperately need.

Nevertheless, there has been some communal progress; I have put forward my ideas, not only to hold a memorial for Joanne one year on after her passing but also to use that as a catalyst for launching a local group to support victims of bullying and abuse. There are a number of charities I intend to speak to as well. Maybe I can encourage someone to come along to the memorial to talk to people about their own experiences.

I feel committed to this project. But first steps. Abigail, from the gardening group, has been so helpful with the media side of things. She is much more computer savvy and has set up a "go fund me" site to raise money in her name for charity. There is a cost to everything but it's such a good feeling to see how positively people are reacting to this appeal. I believe its popularity has gathered some momentum from the favoured "me too" campaign.

On my way home from Sue's, I noticed Abigail busy planting in the square's communal garden. I stopped for a chat, took advantage of the welcome shade provided by the large silver birch tree now clothed in its summer greenery. Abigail told me that with June already here any frost danger has passed. "Time to get the summer annuals in while we are enjoying such lovely weather," she said. Happy to stop for a chat as she had already planted many blue lobelia, white alyssum and red geraniums. With many still to plant, I offered to help tomorrow. We had a chuckle regarding the garden's patriotic appearance. I had donated the Robinia shrubs some time ago, which were now flourishing. We agreed red summer foliage and white flowers would complement the annuals. "But for the geraniums," Abigail said, "I have raised the rest from seed." Such a lovely lady – a fellow green-fingered gardener! As I was leaving, I said, "After our gardening stint tomorrow afternoon you must come to mine for a cuppa and try my home-made lemon drizzle cake. She seemed pleased with the invitation.

It has now been confirmed there will be a Joanne memorial on 13th October. We have been in touch with Joanne's family who, unsurprisingly, have moved away. No response yet but we hope they and *most* of the inhabitants of the square will be in attendance. Since my arrival, some forty years ago, there have been many changes. Mirroring society in general we have witnessed a much more varied and cosmopolitan group of neighbours. Somehow, I believe the postman at number 2 will ignore this service if his total disinterest is anything to go by. Although since he moved that lovely young woman – Ruby, is it? – and her even more delightful son, he does seem to be more amenable to community offerings. I always thought he hid away but I have seen him chatting to people more and he was even buying an ice cream from Dimitri's van the other day, for the child.

I wonder if the "good" doctor will grace us with his presence. I have a feeling not. We shall see, my opinion entirely. Otherwise, my neighbour on the opposite side, Mr Drake, will, I believe, attend. He knew Joanne personally. It was his black labrador, going by the name of Mr Tibbs, that Joanne often walked; she loved that dog! I am comfortable in acknowledging his presence should we pass in the street, which occasionally happens when he is out for his morning jog. Otherwise, I keep my distance having heard that he engages in cage fighting and goes by the name of Calcutta. Whether that is assumed, chosen to suit his

117

fighting activities, I have no idea, but I automatically shy away from anybody or anything violence related.

We must advertise the memorial further afield, nearer to the time. We must not forget that Joanne was a member of a greater community, so we must also reach out to her school and beyond. Depending on our success there is no limit to the good we can deliver. It is my hope that the memorial is merely the start.

To assist Abigail, I have drafted a notice from which we can advertise the event. I do so hope we are successful. Even my involvement this far has improved my own outlook. Maybe it's the idea that I will be helping others in difficult circumstances that makes me feel slightly less anxious. Or maybe it's because I will be helping others *while also* permanently laying to rest my own insecurities.

And so, I gratefully accept my destiny.

The Secret Diary of Joanne Wilson – aged 14 years, 10 months and 3 days

The loom of destiny weaves threads unknown.
— J.D. Salinger, The Catcher in the Rye

No one really sees me. No one but Jack. So tomorrow I'll do it – I'll send it.

Just for your eyes, just for you, Jack. You're the kind of boy a girl would kill herself over.

July
Number 1
Dimitri

I look proudly at my shiny, recently resprayed, ice-cream van, gleaming brilliant yellow in the midday sunshine.

All I have to do now is ensure the ice cream supplies are sufficiently restocked and I'll be ready to go. As well as the best ice cream in the area we always cater to the changing tastes of London with fruity flavours, choc-ices, ice lollies, wafers and flakes. And of course, my special selection of Italian gelato. I love this part of the day, getting ready for the daily round, wondering what will be popular today. Couldn't imagine any other job, a simple honest living. I'd never been the office type or the factory type. Though... there always was the other dream...

My daughter, Lucinda, is on school holidays so has kindly offered to help serve customers; the lad who used to do it has a job in the city now. When I see Lucinda still has not appeared I think it's *less of the kindly* offer and more of the *reluctant, needs the pocket money* offer to help. Still, it'll be good for her – us. I hope. But where is the girl when you need her?

"Come on, Lucinda, get a move on..."

"Coming, Papa, give me a sec!" she bellows from inside the house, front door of number 1 still ajar.

Mama mia, what's keeping her?

Final checks done, I call out again.

This time no answer.

What's she doing in there?

So I sit, hands on the steering wheel and I wait.

And wait.

And wait some more.

Maybe I need to play the tune to get her out here...?

120

But since thoughts these days tend to drift, the next minute here I am thinking about life... Grandpa... where it all started. I've had my round a long time now. I remember when I took over the business – felt like I'd won the lottery. Used to be me serving customers while Grandpa drove. He was the one who started the business... which is why, with a decision to make, one that's kept me from sleep these past few days, I have been pondering so deeply on the past. I should be honouring Grandpa's legacy, but... well, as I say, I have a decision to make. But is it just folly... or can I really have the success I've been promised? You see I have another passion, not just ice cream. I do love to sing. Mostly in the shower, mind. But, well, last month I entered a local talent contest, more on a whim to be fair. It was only at the White Hart pub. I forgot how much I liked to sing and next thing there I was. Once I opened my mouth, closed my eyes, I pretended I was in my bathroom, not in that room with all those people gawping. You could say I was lost in the moment... or few moments as it happens. When I opened my eyes to rapturous applause, I was sure someone famous must've walked in. But seemed it was for me and what's more I'd attracted a lot of attention. They asked for more. So, I gave them four more songs. Some even stood to applaud me. Next thing some guy, a talent scout apparently, was offering to manage me. Hasn't stopped texting since, *you should go on tour, Dimitri! The Singing Ice Cream man. With that tenor voice!* And with my Italian heritage he seems to think it's a new take on *One Cornetto!* Paul Potts eat your heart out. He'd have me on *Britain's Got Talent* next.

So now I'm in a quandary.

I mean, how could I run the business and *go on tour*? It's crazy. A preposterous idea.

Or is it?

Didn't Grandpa say you should always follow your heart, like those ice cream dreams of his… but aren't they mine too? Well, I thought they were.

Still imagining a whole other life, I don't realise Lucinda is now standing on the driveway and would you believe hands on her hips, ripped jeans, DM boots, what is it with her? And *the look* like I've been the one holding her up for the last few minutes. Next thing she's jumping up beside me. She looks more like her mother every day – even the attitude. *Especially* the attitude.

"Ready?" she says.

"Almost."

It seems every time I think about the offer, the new life, Grandpa gets into my head. With that, I gently tease my wallet from the back pocket of my jeans and open it, look at the creased old photograph of Grandpa. I remove it and stick on the dashboard in front of us. Lucinda proffers a wry smile.

"I am ready now," I mumble. As if on cue the phone in my other pocket beeps. I don't even need to look to know it's him again, *when am I gonna go and meet him… sign up for a once-in-a-lifetime offer. The Singing Ice Cream Man.* But if I go, I won't be an ice cream man any more, will I?

"Papa?"

"Yeah, let's go sell ice cream!"

As we pull off Station Square (we'll be back later, not busy at this time) I switch on the tune and let the sound drown out everything else… especially my dilemma. The last message said he'd waited for long enough, if I didn't let him know today, he'd assume I got cold feet. Cold feet? In July? No, it wasn't that. This was about Grandpa. And ice cream.

Something about children's smiles always shifts a bad mood. Today's no exception. And summer is always a busy time. I

122

watch Lucinda and even she seems to have got into the swing of it now. I mean all teenagers are moody, Lucinda included, but working together, like this, well it makes me appreciate it, family businesses you know. And since her mama left, she only has me; I only have her. Time seems to float by like it did when I used to help Grandpa: Pudding Lane, Blackberry Way, Blackthorn Road, School Lane… our tune tinkling away to herald our arrival – ice-cream smiles all around on our carefully planned route. Grandpa used to love this. So do I.

Finally, we need a break and to top up, we've had a run on ice lollies… the ones shaped like mobile phones though Lucinda reckons they're rockets. Really? Hard to predict the trends but I like to keep the customer happy. We need to head back to Station Square. I like to keep to the clock; people have learned the schedule and if I'm too early or too late they'll tell me so.

It's as I pull into the square, I see him.

Blood seems to freeze in my veins like the ice cream in the pipes. He's wearing a *Dr Who* T-shirt, jeans, his hands are in his pockets. He's standing gazing up at number 11, the other side of the square to our house. I know who he is; I've seen him before.

His name, I believe, is Jack Henderson.

Number 11 is the house Joanne lived in. The girl who… *died…* last October. I pull around the corner, go past the communal garden and onto the driveway of number 1. Didn't see where the boy went, though I can still see him in my head. I see him as I did last summer, buying an ice cream for Joanne – a 99 – her favourite. Only it looked like they'd had some kind of argument, as kids do I suppose – never really thought much of it – until in a temper he threw her ice cream on the ground. I didn't see where they went after that because next thing that fighter bloke – Calcutta

Drake, I mean what kind of name is that – came along and all I saw was that black labrador of his lapping up Joanne's ice cream.

I immediately messaged Lucinda in the house, since she knew her and asked her to take her another 99 and see if she was okay. You see I liked Joanne, reminded me a lot of Lucinda – both keen students. Not sure if she ever said what happened; I think she used to talk to Lucinda, about stuff, boys I suppose though I never was too sure about the boy Joanne was hanging about with. Seems my instincts were right.

There's been a lot of talk of bullying and that Joanne did what she did because the boy was a bully but this is not like any bullying I've known.

Lucinda showed me the photograph.

The one he sent everywhere.

They talk about photos going viral and I never really knew what that meant. But seems Joanne, such a bright kid, did what she thought was normal – sent a photo in private to her boyfriend. Now I know what viral means. They call it cyberbullying, what happened after that. Another thing I looked up on Google to try to understand. You should have seen the terrible things people said about her and *that* photo. I only saw some of them but the names they called her. They even said things like *why don't you kill yourself?* Did they really mean that? Is that why she… *Mama Mia*. Surely not. It was a photo sent in innocence. Bare breasts; but no mistaking her face in the picture. That *boyfriend* thought it was okay to share it. Lucinda said she heard it was meant to be a joke sent to one mate and he then shared it with a mate but however it happened it should never have gone further than the lad she sent it to. I think it happened right before the schools shut for the summer, and blew right up when she went back in September. Before she knew it, everyone in school and, way beyond that, had seen it and had an opinion about her.

I wish I knew where the boy's gone now. Probably down the alleyway. What a thing to do to that poor girl. I told Lucinda, don't you ever do what she did – you can trust no one. I look at Lucinda now as we restock the ice lollies.

I mean look at me, I'm Italian, we speak the language of love and I know a thing or two about passion. But it was different in my day and if there was such a thing as a saucy photo, even if you did show a mate, that's as far as it could ever go.

Social media has a lot to answer for. I am only on Instagram because Lucinda put me on there, for the business. When I think about bloody Jack Henderson – *Mama mia*. I'd never sell him an ice cream again. Where's he go? Then I think, do you ever really know what your kids are doing?

Lucinda doesn't have a boyfriend yet – but she will. Soon enough. Seen her making eyes at that Adrian boy though she says they're only friends; he's older and she feels better talking to him – about what happened, about Joanne. He'd been good friends with Joanne. At least she's talking to someone.

And she'd never do what Joanne did, send photos like that to a boy, she's a good girl.

But then so was Joanne.

By the time we reach Gravenor Square the talent scout has texted three more times about the approaching deadline and there are two missed calls. No doubt another voice message too. I need to decide. I mean, at my age this could be my last chance. He seems to think the offer's better than *X-Factor*, *BGT*. We'll see...

Now we do Mile End, Rushbottom Lane, Mornington Park...

It's when we pass the White Hart pub, I think about how

125

singing makes me feel and is that truly my calling? I mean…

We pull over for a short tea break.

"Papa?"

When I look at Lucinda, she's fingering the strings on her guitar. She sometimes keeps it in the van. I don't think she knows I have a decision to make, but she does know how well the singing went and I've told her what I sung. Next thing there she is playing and there I am singing. It's the happiest I am, truly… happiness is hard to know, let alone keep; I only have to think about my marriage to realise that. So if it makes me this happy maybe it's not so whimsical imagining making a living from it? I mean, I did get a standing ovation. I sing *It's Now or Never*, *Sweet Surrender*, *Suspicion*. And like last time I am lost. When I look up it seems the van has drawn quite a crowd at the bottom of Rushbottom Lane, and I don't mean for ice cream.

Inside my head I hear a voice: *sign the deal, what have you got to lose?*

What have I got to lose?

When we finally finish the last street and head home, the sun kissing the sky pink and orange, I think maybe I will give *him* a call, might be worth at least discussing terms? How long will I have to be away from home though? Lucinda can't… I will just have to do local gigs. If it's meant to be it will happen – another one of Grandpa's sayings. I pick up his photograph from the dashboard of the ice cream van and look at him – we look similar, same eyes, same cheeky smile. "What do I do, Grandpa?"

Life is full of uncertainty. I think it now as I look at Lucinda, kicking off her DM boots and flopping onto the sofa. Her mama was so disappointed when she was born.

She wanted a boy. What did it matter? Last we heard she'd used her divorce settlement to go to the south of France. Good riddance. But then again, my own parents were not the best parents – I never felt their love; I vowed to not be like them. That's why, as a kid, Grandpa ended up taking care of me. I was bullied but Grandpa taught me to stand up to them. And he was the one who encouraged my singing when he knew I had a voice – took me to the local church. That's when life changed for me.

Was that the start of this dream of mine?

As I stand at the window, look across the square, another day wearing out, I pull the curtain across and wonder what it must have been like for that poor girl's parents. When something like that happens, you can't help wondering if there was something you could have done. I wonder what she dreamed of being. Lucinda said she had plans to go to uni. What a terrible waste of a young life.

Grandpa said you can be anything you want to be – that was when he talked of ice cream – gelato – from back home where he was born, in Italy. How he'd dream in ice cream. And he passed that passion onto me.

So should I do it?

Give it up for the dream?

I reach into my pocket, tease out my phone and wonder. Do I call? Say I'll do it, give it all up on a whim?

"Papa?"

I look across to see Lucinda spawled on the sofa. "What, love?"

"I really enjoyed today. I think I understand what you mean when you say how you love making people smile. I mean, who doesn't like ice cream?"

I could name a few miserable buggers, but I don't.

"So you'll help throughout the summer holidays?"

"Yeah. Why not? For free ice cream."

I laugh, fumble with my phone and its unread messages. "Dream big, Luce, it's a summer job for a bright girl like you. You can be anything; like Joanne could have, but… well…"

"I know, Papa"

With that, I gently tease back the edge of the green curtain and look out at my van, resprayed, it looks buttery yellow in the moonlight and I think, "I love this life. How can I leave all this?"

With that I poke my phone back into my pocket and think instead about tomorrow. I can still be the Singing Ice Cream Man, if Lucinda keeps bringing her guitar. I can still do it… only my way.

"Papa?"

"Yeah?"

"Fancy a panzanella salad?"

"Yeah, let's make it together."

And with that, we go into the kitchen, and I think I need to order more of those mobile or rocket ice lollies – you never can predict the trends.

Nor should you stop doing what makes you happy. If Joanne taught us all one thing, it's people can be cruel and life really is too short. Who needs some talent agent at my age when I can sell the best ice cream in London? And sing my way through the streets?

And that, I decide, is exactly what I'll do.

The Secret Diary of Joanne Wilson – aged 14 years, 10 months and 5 days

Power does not ask permission.
            — **J.D. Salinger, The Catcher in the Rye**

What have I done? What have you done? Another piece of me chiselled away by their cruel remarks and perceptions... I give up.

August
Number 11
Schu

My husband and I are the current residents of number 11 Station Square. He's Simon Bradford and I'm Simon Schuster – that's right, we're both called Simon – but I go by Schu, a nickname I've had all my life to which I'm quite attached. That's because it probably saves me from a slew of assault charges but, while that might sound a bit odd, once you know that being introduced as Simon Schuster gives people a vague feeling they've heard the name before – even those who wouldn't know what a book was if it hit them over the head – they always ask if I'm famous or something. That's inevitably followed with a conversation about how funny it must be. I've spent most of my adult life answering the same questions, usually through gritted teeth, because the constant repetition gets old, really, really fast. Another reason is that it avoids the mix-ups that would undoubtedly occur if both Simon and I answered to the same name. If you think about it, I guess being known as Schu is probably what keeps me sane.

So, why haven't I changed it? It's crossed my mind of course – but firstly, I didn't want to upset my old man; secondly, I'm a bit of a lazy sod and really couldn't be bothered with all the faff and lastly, I guess I probably thought that when I met that special someone, I'd take his name and the problem would go away. Big "however" here though – in that subtle way the universe has of letting you know who's really in charge – the love of my life was also called Simon and that idea went right out of the window. So, Simon gets to keep his name; I'm more than happy to be known as Schu and our friends just call us "the Simons".

Anyway, I'm a consultant in IT and a lot of the time I work from home and no – that doesn't mean I sit on my arse all day playing computer games. I'm a proper, technical person: the go-to guy when things go wrong and I'm very good at what I do. Over my career, I've built up quite a reputation in the industry and I even publish the odd article in the technical press. I did grow up with computers though – my dad was into them in the very early days and I was using them as a little kid – I think he bought a program that taught me to type when I was about three, so the fact that the various degrees I hold are all in the subject isn't that surprising. I suppose you could say it's in my blood and certainly it's always played a large part in my life.

The square is in London's east end – but our real home's in northern Italy. About six or seven years ago, we bought an old villa in the small town of Bobbio, which is roughly half-way between Milan and Genoa. It's an absolutely beautiful place and it's very, very old. We're really happy there but unfortunately, my dad got sick late last year, so we had to close up the villa and come back to England.

Finding number 11 was a huge stroke of luck.

The house has a nice aspect – it's at the end of a row situated on a square with a gated communal garden in the centre. The area's not bad at all and the bonus is that it's close to my parents, so it seemed fortuitous when it turned out that the family who owned the house had already moved out and were looking to rent it as soon as. Fully furnished too. The agent told us that they'd gone to live in their second home, which I assumed was a holiday place or something, presumably closer to where they needed to be in a hurry. I'm guessing they must have had good reason for not wanting to sell the house outright – the agent did say something about a family emergency – but I didn't ask as we never actually met them and it was none of my business anyway. Besides, not to sound too callous, the circumstances were so favourable to us that I thought it best not to poke about too much.

Having to leave the villa and come home for an indeterminate period, though, had been a bit of a wrench but as things were, we couldn't really have done anything else. It's fortunate that I have a cartload of relatives living in Bobbio so at least I knew somebody would be keeping an eye on the place while we were away; and my cousin pops over and flicks a duster round every so often.

As a kid, I spent a lot of time holidaying with the cousins, so I know the area really well. When me and Simon were contemplating leaving London for somewhere cheaper, I recalled this old villa from my childhood visits. Granted, it was a bit of a radical idea because northern Italy was a tad further outside of London than we'd had in mind but given that an IT consultant can more or less live anywhere he wants, it began to seem like a viable proposition. So, we took a few days to pop over and take a look and fit in a visit to my cousins at the same time. In the end I probably wasn't really surprised to find that the villa I remembered had long since been renovated and sold but one of my cousins said he knew of another place – roughly fifteen minutes out of town – which was available. He said he'd take us over for a look if we were interested.

This other villa had been empty for a long time and needed a lot of work but the first glimpse sold it to us, even before we'd seen the inside. Enrico knew the owner and filled us in on the history – apparently, the old lady who owned it had left to live with her daughter several years ago but she hadn't wanted it to go to some foreign developer and therefore it had never been actively marketed. My family connections and the time I'd spent in the area as a kid apparently meant I'd be viewed as a local boy, so any offer from us was very likely to be accepted.

I think, despite the amount of work needed, we could already see ourselves making a home there and, once we looked at the figures and worked out that it was still cheaper than anything we could afford in the UK, it was a no-brainer. The added advantage with the helping hands in the form of all my local relatives didn't hurt either.

So, how did I come to be related to a large clan of Italians living in a small town in the north of Italy? Well, it's where my nanna grew up and, as the story goes, she met my grandpa when he was bombing around Italy on a motor bike back in the fifties. Apparently, he rounded a bend going far too fast (according to Nanna) and only just avoided knocking her down. At some point they managed to stop shouting at each other long enough to fall in love and were married within weeks. I suspect the truth is probably a little more prosaic but it's a good story and that's what makes family history. Sadly, beautiful views don't fill empty bellies and there wasn't enough work locally to support them, so they were forced to leave Bobbio and move to England. My mum was born a couple of years later and though there's always been loads of contact with her Italian relatives, she really grew up in England and spent her whole life there; so I'd imagine that that's home for her as it's certainly what she's used to.

Anyway, here we are living back in the UK and while I won't say finding number 11 was anything other than a real stroke of luck, when we first arrived, it wasn't a whole lot of fun either. First off, Simon needed a job. Moving back didn't affect my work too much, as I've already said, I can work from anywhere, but the UK isn't cheap and we needed a second income to pay the bills. There were the agents and the lease on this place to deal with, not to mention the move itself, so we were relieved that the place came furnished even if it wasn't to our taste. Fitting that in while still finding the time to go and see my dad every day and making sure my mum was okay was more than just a little difficult – not to mention that I did still have a job to do – I just didn't stop. Sadly, my dad passed away a few months after we got back; so then there were funeral arrangements and all the probate and legal stuff to sort through for Mum – which is still ongoing by the way – and on top of all that I had my own grief to cope with but time moves on and things have started to settle down a bit – sometimes I have a whole five minutes to myself – ha ha. Seriously, though, I'm finding that I can, at last, start to take stock and think about the future. To be brutally honest, while we were always going to head back to Italy at some point, I'd prefer if it were sooner rather than later, but of course, there's Mum – I don't feel I can just swan off and leave her alone; and then there's the lease on this place. We took it for a year originally so there's probably about three months or so left; can I wrap everything up in that time or should we extend it?

An IT consultant might be *able* to live anywhere but that doesn't necessarily mean it's always possible. It would be nice if I could persuade Mum to come back to Italy with us, but I don't know – it would be a huge upheaval for her – and although she does have relatives in the area, would she be ready to go and live there? I'll need to think about that. Simon and I have talked about it, but it's not really going to be our decision.

On the plus side Simon did find a job. He still had contacts in the city from before we left which helped and as we're both fluent in Italian he landed a fairly decent position as a broker in an Italian-owned investment firm. It didn't hurt that the salary was pretty good and he does seem to be getting on very nicely. Only fly in the ointment, from my point of view, is the number of times he's worked late over the past few weeks. We've not spoken about it but I'm guessing "working late" means they're all popping down the pub for a drink and while I understand the ethos and that he does need to fit in, I'm not sure I'm happy about it. For one thing, it's not really like him and it does seem to be happening more often than I'd like. Maybe that's another conversation we need to have.

Oh, and that brings us to the problems we had with the neighbours when we first came to live here. Being a fairly affable sort of bloke, it wasn't something I expected, but after we moved in, we thought it might be a good idea to invite them all round so they could see that the Simons were perfectly ordinary and as normal as everybody else. As Christmas was on the horizon, a festive drinks evening seemed like a really good idea; so we printed invites, poked them inside Christmas cards, and walked round and posted them through everybody's letter box. There we were, on the appointed night, all dressed up in our stupid Christmas jumpers – we were even wearing Santa hats. There was the ubiquitous tree complete with star, twinkling away in the corner and a table with legs bowing under the weight of the best Sainsbury's had to offer, an enormous fancy Christmas cake and a dish bearing a huge pile of sliced lemons waiting hopefully for a drink to come along and give them purpose. They had taken me bloody ages to cut up.

We stood there waiting, wearing our brightest, most welcoming smiles, and nobody – not one single person – turned up. They didn't even bother to let us know. Of course, I was convinced it was because we were a gay couple and that we'd probably failed some sort of approval test but while it might not be that unusual to find a homophobic attitude with some of the older folk, I really didn't expect it from the younger guys. Then again, there's no accounting for folk so perhaps I shouldn't have been surprised. I was furious at the snub though, and I thought if they're going to write off the Simons without even getting to know us, then sod 'em. I even went to the trouble of buying pink curtains and hanging them in the living room windows as a way of giving them the finger, but Simon – always the voice of reason – said they were awful and the gesture was pointless as nobody would know why we'd done it. Once I'd calmed down a bit, I had to agree he was right. Still at least it eventually gave us something to laugh about and lord knows we needed that.

Despite what I said to Simon, it still bothered me though because I found myself thinking about it over the following days. I work from home, so I dress for comfort – jeans, T-shirts and trainers – that sort of thing – but I don't wear any old rubbish, I can afford decent stuff, after all I'm not seventeen anymore; but then again, as I don't really care that much about clothes and fashion I guess I can maybe look a little rumpled sometimes and I s'pose that might matter to some. Simon, on the other hand, is perfectly well turned out – booted and suited during the week and smart casual at weekends and you'd never catch him wearing trainers with the sole hanging off so I'm pretty sure that can't be the reason we were boycotted. It's not even as if they'd been subjected to any of the more flamboyant members of our circle because, due to how busy we'd been, the normal get-togethers and dinner parties that would have seen our friends paying us a visit hadn't happened, which did make it a little strange. Eventually, I put it down to bigotry and intolerance and decided that they just weren't worth the bother and I had to let it go. I thought we should just ignore them and as a result, we had as little to do with the neighbours as possible, which meant, of course, we missed anything that might have been going on in the neighbourhood. But I have to say, it still irks me that no one came to our do but è la vita – as we'd say in Italian.

I glance at my watch surprised at how late it is. Walking over to the window, I gaze across at the square. No sign of Simon and, as I've been stuck indoors all day and could do with stretching my legs, I decide to take a stroll over to the offy and pick up a couple of bottles of wine. Grabbing my wallet and phone, I shrug on a jacket and head for the front door.

As I'm heading back towards the square on my way home, I see the ice cream van pull onto the driveway of number 1. I've seen the van around a few times and although we have tried their ice cream. They do an excellent vanilla and the tutti frutti is out of this world according to Simon. I don't really know the guy. So now I'm wondering if I should buy some ice cream and use it as an opportunity to introduce myself. Maybe this could be a good way to build some bridges and perhaps move on from the disaster that had been Christmas.

I change direction to catch up with the van and, as I stand and wait, the bloke who runs the van gets out followed by a teenage girl. I hear him speak to the girl in Italian so – on a whim – I decide to introduce myself using my Italian.

"Excuse me," I say (in Italian) "I realise you're probably at the end of your round but I'm Simon Schuster from number 11 over on the other side of the square and I wondered if you had a tub of vanilla ice cream I could buy?"

The man looks puzzled. "That name rings a bell," he says. "Are you famous?"

I resist the urge to punch him in the face. "I think it's probably just a really common name," I say through gritted teeth.

He holds out his hand. "Dimitri," he says and, pointing at the girl, "my daughter Lucinda. You speak very good Italian."

"My grandmother's Italian and I've just returned to the UK after living out there for a few years."

He asks me where my family were from and where I'd been living in Italy and when I tell him his face lights up. "Oh, I know Bobbio – it's the place with that ancient bridge." He shakes my hand vigorously. "We're almost neighbours, I'm originally from Bardi about an hour and a half away."

He seems delighted to meet somebody who was practically a fellow countryman and invites me in. He apologises that there isn't any ice cream left on board the van but says he has some in his freezer store. "Come, come – come in for tea," he says and I happily accept.

He shows me into the living room and after a short time his daughter appears bearing tea and biscuits. She hands me a cup and sits down on the arm of the sofa across from the coffee table.

"You're one of the blokes who moved into Joanne's house, aren't you?"

I ask if Joanne is one of the Wilson children and explain that I don't know the family as we went through the agents after they moved out so haven't actually met them. She says yes and I nod and tell her that we moved in last November.

"D'you mind if I ask," Lucinda says, "but did you put up the pink curtains because of Joanne, because it was her favourite colour?"

I am a bit taken aback as it's a very strange question, but given that the real reason for putting the curtains up makes me look like a dick, I make up something on the spur of the moment about it being all we had that fitted that window and I say, "Oh, I expect the pink room must have been Joanne's then."

138

Lucinda says it was and when I ask her if she'd been friendly with Joanne, she nods and says they were very good friends.

"It must be hard now she's gone – I expect you probably miss her."

Lucinda inhales sharply and stands up abruptly. She rushes out of the room mumbling something I don't catch.

I stare after her and then turn to Dimitri. "Is she okay? She seems a little upset at my question. Did I say something wrong?"

Dimitri stares at me for a long moment. "You don't know do you?"

"Know what?"

He then tells me what happened last year and about the memorial service that's being organised for the anniversary in October.

"Joanne was a nice girl so everybody around the square was affected to some degree or other, but the youngsters were hit particularly hard. Lucinda..." he shrugs and lets the end of the sentence tail off.

Realisation suddenly hits me – it's the house the neighbours are avoiding, not us. I say, "I'm so sorry, I had no idea."

I ask him to apologise to Lucinda and tell her I didn't know. Dimitri waves away my apologies and insists on giving me a tub of ice cream for which he refuses to take any payment. We shake hands and I turn to walk home trying to process everything I've just heard.

How could I not have known? But the answer to that comes almost immediately – because I've been so busy looking for slights, I hadn't wanted to know. My condemnation of the neighbourhood had been far too hasty; I hadn't even tried to find out what the problems were. I feel bad; I must have looked so rude and standoffish and I want to put things right.

Dimitri spoke of the memorial service being organised. Maybe I can help with that – make it truly memorable. I have contacts from all walks of life and know people who could make things happen. Of course, I will have to speak to the organisers but maybe I can help make it a real occasion – a special memorial – and make up for my previous attitude.

I'm turning all this over in my head as I walk across the square when I glance up and see Simon heading towards me.

"Hello, big guy, all on your own?" he says giving me a lascivious wink.

Responding to one of the silly jokes that we often use between us, I hold up my hands in mock horror and reply, "No, no, I'm a happily married man."

We both laugh and he asks me where I've been and I hold up the bag containing the wine and ice cream. He says he has something we need to talk about and he directs me towards the bench. We sit down and I wait for him to speak. He looks so serious I start to feel a wee bit apprehensive.

"So, you know I've been working late a bit lately."

"More than a bit."

"Yeah well, actually, I haven't really been working late," Simon says.

I don't say anything but my heart rate increases.

Simon takes a deep breath and continues. "I've actually been taking part in a few meetings – well, a lot of meetings really, with my directors. The upshot is that they want to open a new office in Italy and have finally decided on Piacenza."

I'm gobsmacked. "But that's only about a fifty-minute drive from Bobbio."

"Well, they've now confirmed that they'd like me to head it up," Simon says, "and best of all, as there's still quite a bit of organising to do, the opening isn't likely to be before we've returned to Bobbio, although I might occasionally have to travel over there during the set up."

"Simon, that's absolutely amazing. I thought you were spending your time in the pub."

"Yeah – I couldn't say anything until it was definite because I didn't want to get your hopes up in case it all fell through; but I received confirmation late this afternoon and I rushed home to tell you. Think about it, it's absolutely perfect. We can go home to Bobbio and the cherry on the top is that there'll be a few days a week when I can work from home."

I'm delighted, and itching to tell him what I'd learned about Joanne and my ideas for the memorial, but that can wait until later.

I say, "Let's go home and order in – get something nice to go with the wine and then perhaps we should give my mum a ring; see how she feels about coming to live in Italy with us."

"Ah yeah – that's the other thing," Simon says. "I really hope you don't mind but I knew you were worried about your mum and weren't sure how to raise the subject, so I jumped in and spoke to her for you. I also wanted her to know that I wanted her there with us as well. Now that your dad's gone, I thought she'd be far better off coming to live with us – home is where your family is after all. Anyway, I'm happy to report that she seemed quite taken with the idea. She said she could think of nothing better than being able to take care of her boys."

"Mr Bradford, I think I could kiss you," I say. "I don't think I've felt this happy since our wedding day."

Simon grins. "Maybe not here in the park, though," he says, "after all we don't want to set the neighbours off again."

We stand up and he takes my hand. "This will have to do until later," he says, "I'm starving, let's go home and get our food sorted and maybe you could call your mum while we're waiting."

As we stroll through the growing shadows of early evening the rays of the setting sun shine on the windows of our house giving it a homely glow. It feels like a good omen and maybe, after the year we've had, this is a sign that everything is going to work out just fine.

The Secret Diary of Joanne Wilson – aged 14 years, 10 months and 1 week

I think, even, if I ever die, and they stick me in a cemetery, and I have a tombstone and all, it'll say "Holden Caulfield" on it, and then what year I was born and what year I died, and then right under that it'll say "Fuck you."
                    — J.D. Salinger, The Catcher in the Rye

They've all seen. I think I shall plan my death.

September
Number 3
Abigail

Little streams, wet and glistening, roll down the front window.

They fall one way then another; they come together then part. Like life. Different paths, different directions. And in the blink of an eyelid, it can all be over.

The silver birch has already started its metamorphosis. Puts me in mind of a small dog after a walk in the rain, like it shakes itself from head to tail and the colour changes from green to brown, top to bottom.

Why is life so complicated? Simple at times but that's if it all runs smoothly.

I remember being late, rushing and then even getting on the wrong train, always in a hurry. Now I have to take life more slowly and concentrate.

Mum would say you're like a butterfly, never settling down and trying to taste every bit of nectar, every little drop and going from one thing to another in case it was better.

Settle down, Abbey, for once in your life, she would say. It's almost sixty years ago but I can still hear her voice.

I was full of life then, without a care in the world, and without aches and pains.

I wanted to try everything then. I even tried drugs. Poor Mum was devastated. I still want to run through the fields, the freedom I felt would overwhelm me and I would feel the sun glistening on my long hair as I ran and would fall into a haystack and giggle at life.

"Are you on that wacky baccy, Abbey?" Mum would say just because I would laugh at the smallest of things.

Terry, you came to my rescue, my knight in shining armour. I couldn't take my eyes of you at the village hall youth club. The following Saturday I was walking through the bluebell wood and you followed me into the field on your bike. You shouted after me to come and sit and talk for a while; you kissed me then and I never wanted to be away from you from that very moment. I was fifteen. Our love was so strong. A tear rolls down, miss you so much, Terry. I stroke Milly who has decided to sit on my lap.

Oh, to be fifteen again.

But when I think that, I think how some people don't even get to fifteen.

I glance out of the window; it's stopped raining again but I see a dark cloud coming over. I guess I had better get the washing in before it gets more wet than when I put it out. If I use the tumble dryer it will eat the pennies up. The red top you bought me is waving in the breeze with the sheets and towels.

That reminds me: red top. I need some more red top milk; I forgot to get it last time. I wonder if I subconsciously forget so it gives me something to go out for later or the next day.

They are not really dry yet but I fold them neatly into the basket.

I think of all the dolls in Maisie's window, all facing out as if looking at what's going on in the outside world, trapped in their dolly brains, a little like me I guess, searching for happiness.

Shall I venture out now? I think not as I'm still a bit snuffly from my last walk out.

I turn the radio up as it's just too silent. I feel particularly lonely today and if I'm not reminiscing about Terry then I'm thinking of Joanne.

Love Me Tender comes on. I look across at Terry's photo and wink at it as if he can see me.

You have been out of my life for twenty years and a day doesn't go by where I don't think of you. I reach out for our wedding photo and the one next to it on our trip to Thailand. Yes, we loved each other very much.

That day was just like any other day. You walked into the kitchen and you suddenly clasped your chest and fell. All so dramatic, the kind of thing you see on the TV. I held you for a long time, head in my lap stroking your face, wet with my tears but I knew it was too late. You left me too soon.

I wanted to join you but I guess it wasn't my time. I think of young Joanne; it certainly wasn't her time either.

I spend my days living my life through others, people-watching out of the window. I do go out of course to break the monotony, just to Mark's paper shop; that's where I first met Joanne. I remember I was trying to carry a paper, tins of cat food for Milly and a big bar of chocolate. I slipped on a loose paving slab and she helped me up. She asked me if I lived locally and I said I only live up the road and she took me back home and bathed my knee.

You were a good girl, Joanne, kind and caring.

She called the next day to see how I was; noticed my fuchsias and roses in the back garden. It surprised me when she asked if she could look at my flowers. She said she didn't have a very pretty garden as her brother Jimmy played football and flattened everything.

"Can I help you sometimes in the garden, please?" she said and I said of course, never really expecting her to come back, but she appeared a week later after school and said she had come to help me. These days kids aren't like that – she was a good one.

146

I really looked forward to her visits and we would talk about different plants; she remembered a lot of their names too and even said she wouldn't mind working in a garden centre.

I said, "Joanne, I'm sure you'll get a better job."

"While I'm at uni then," she said.

We talked about school and her friends and boys and she reminded me of my younger days. She loved English literature. She always had her head in one book or the other.

She introduced me to her grandad Bert; he was visiting from Cumbria for a few months. I think maybe he knew loneliness too. I liked Bert a lot and we got on really well, he even came to bingo at the British legion with me, and she brought him round for tea and cakes.

Maisie next door, now she's a funny bugger, but there when I need her, she's a diamond. She laughed when she saw Bert.

"Oh, Abigail," she said. "I've seen a change in you lately." And she winked at me. She is a fortune teller, reads the tea leaves, bless her.

I have a daughter Susie who said she would always be there for me, when Terry died suddenly, but within six months she moved away. Michael had been offered a good job in Newcastle and off she went. I remember her saying, "Mum, we can have more quality time together; you can stay up at ours and we can always stay with you too."

First it was okay and I stayed a couple of times, but I gradually realised they had their own lives and I felt in the way. Somewhere along life's path you become… spare.

Autumn and Shane, my grandchildren, led busy lives: football, netball, dancing, cricket etc., so when I went there, they had to go here there, everywhere! We never did much together. Now I have a life here such as it is. Joanne just didn't realise how much her company meant to me.

147

I need to get out more, go for long walks before the winter sets in.

I did pop out a bit earlier; that's when I saw all Maisie's dolls lined up in the window, a strange character but lovely too. I also looked at the communal garden earlier, and thought of all the bulbs I put in there, mainly ones that I had separated from my own garden. I thought of Terry when I planted anything, wishing he could see them shooting through the earth welcoming spring. Now it's September and nearly a year has gone by since Joanne did what she did.

I have planted a lot in the communal garden, forget-me-nots and hardy fuchsias. She would have liked them.

As I sit with my coffee and paper I glance out of the window and see the postman next door. I see he's home earlier today but later he will go out and come back late at night; when he slams his gate shut, he wakes me up although I'm a light sleeper anyway. I wonder what he's up to. Maisie thinks he's up to no good though there is a woman and child living there now and I said he did smile at me. "Maybe he isn't so good with people," she said. I guess we never do know what's going on in people's lives. It's easy to judge. He might be going out and doing late-night ballroom dancing or something – like a secret hobby. I doubt it though.

I think about Bert, Joanne's grandad; he did make me laugh, for the first time in years, he and Joanne came round together a few times. She said once that maybe, when he goes home, I can visit him, get a train or something. I smiled. I didn't know what to say. How was Bert now I wondered.

I reminisce again, wonder who will be at the memorial Carol is organising in Joanne's memory. Maybe Bert will come. I did try to talk to him after it happened. I saw him with Jimmy. I think he still went to school, at least for a bit. Normality I suppose – we all seek it, but it will never be normal for that family now, will it. Then they left. No more than a quick goodbye and a hand-wave.

The photo I have of Joanne, Bert and me that she took was a selfie, she said, and it sits on my dresser and I say rest in peace every night to her along with Terry.

I remember Maisie reading our tea leaves at mine. She had a strange look on her face when she looked at Joanne's, "Don't let anyone take that sunshine out of those lovely eyes," she said.

It wasn't that long after that it happened.

I'm not the only one who noticed something change in Joanne. I tried to ask her what was troubling her but she obviously didn't want to tell me anything. I knew it was something she did. I don't understand the technology these youngsters use, though I am quite good on the computer which is why Carol had me typing the invites for the memorial and looking into Go Fund Me pages. I can use Facebook but don't know much about Instagram or Tik Tok or whatever other things the youngsters use. Whatever Joanne did, it seems it was contagious. I don't know what that means, like a disease I suppose. Something viral. I know it was connected with a boy at school she was seeing. I wanted to talk to her parents but they may have thought I was an old busybody with nothing better to do. She had some tablets from the doctor but she never said what they were for. Surely not antidepressants? She was only fourteen. But since the rumours about the doctor on the square, it makes me wonder. You never see him much these days. The surgery's shut I heard.

Things seemed to get even worse when Joanne went back to school; she usually couldn't wait to get back after the

149

holidays. I remember her phone going off and she just turned it over so I couldn't see what she was looking at.

I asked her if anything was worrying her, but she just shook her head.

"It just keeps happening," she said out loud.

"What does, love?" But she just said I was not to worry and she would sort her problem out.

I'm jolted back to the present when there's a knock on the door. I peep out of the curtain and see it's Maisie.

She's standing there in front of me, rain dripping from her – from her long flowery skirt to her bright pink headscarf, tied up in a turban. I smile at her. She always looks like a gypsy.

"You okay, Maisie, you're soaked through?"

"I've locked myself out, what a silly bugger I am. I'm hoping one of the young lads up the road will climb over the fence later when they get home."

I invite her in and it's nice to have some company at last. I make her a cuppa and find a bar of Fruit and Nut to share. "Soon be here won't it, Maisie," I say.

Maisie tries to change the subject and I say about the two men who live at Joanne's old house. "What a funny pair they are," I say. "They're married by the way. Seems we got it wrong, about the being unsympathetic when they invited us to their party, remember? Turns out they didn't know about Joanne. Couldn't've seen it in the paper, or maybe they didn't join the dots. Anyway, I heard from Dimitri – you know the ice cream man – that he put them straight and they are helping with the memorial. Apparently one of them knows someone on the local council. Harriet Smallcroft? And he knows a charity who support this kind of thing. So, the one she spoke to, Boot… I think she said is his nickname…"

"Boot?"

"Or it might be Shoe? Anyway, whoever... he was going to give Carol the name of someone from a local charity who might speak at the memorial. So, turns out they're not so bad." I chuckle. "I'm going to plant a tree in the garden, a rose tree. Joanne loved my roses, said it was like a beautiful expensive perfume. I'm trying to find one with a suitable name like Sunshine or even Lovely Lady or Joanne even."

"Sounds a lovely idea, Abbey."

"Fancy a trip up to Kew Gardens?"

"Yes, that will be just perfect."

"Thanks, Maisie, you've cheered me up. We can't change what has happened but we can try to change the future eh, Maisie?

The Secret Diary of Joanne Wilson – aged 14 years, 11 months, 3 weeks, 6 days

Man's plight is the darkness of his own making...
With decision comes the clarity of control.
— **J.D. Salinger, The Catcher in the Rye**

Nowhere to hide.
No way out.
FAILED.
What I will miss by dying tonight... the possibility
of anything getting better.

October
Number 7
The "Good" Doctor

It's the 13th of October; the greyness of the day reflected in my hair and my mood. Even that tree looks twisted and bare in places now. Won't be long before you can see right the way through it.

It's been a full twelve months since that awful incident; it has touched everyone who lived on the square or who knew the young girl. Everybody responded in a different way, but for me, who was known by everyone, as the "Good" Doctor there was little I could do, little I could say, little I could offer. Words of solace and words of comfort would not bring her back.

In these last twelve months I have often wondered if I missed the warning signs, had I dismissed her symptoms as being those of a "silly young girl"? And these past few months there have been vicious rumours that I let her down. Everyone needs someone to blame.

I sigh and look about at the organised chaos in the House cum Surgery. All around are packing crates, boxes full to bursting, all neatly labelled. Magazines in stacks, secured by heavy string, old copies of *Private Eye, People's Friend*, and *Autocar*; plus, the obligatory medical journals, *Pulse*, the *BMJ* and *Lancet* that spilled out from both the old waiting room and my consulting room into the downstairs hallway.

I wander into the kitchen at the back of the house, which like everywhere else, is awash with boxes, all efficiently labelled by my wife. The kettle, cups, tea caddy, coffee jar and sugar are still on the worktop; the fridge empty except for milk and butter. I make coffee and take it into the old consulting room. I sit in my old well-worn comfortable leather captain's chair. Still in position behind the old antique dark brown mahogany desk, with its dark leather top, now cleared of all the paraphernalia of my previous practice, gone are the diaries, stacks of blood request and X-ray forms, prescription pads and computer. Much of the old consulting room itself is now empty except for the stacks of medical magazines and textbooks that have accumulated over the years, my desk and chair still in the same place they've stood for nearly thirty years. Time passes, and time will heal, but for me retiral now beckons. Some might call it running away; you see I can't shake what happened, how Joanne reached out to me and how... well, I ought to have known better.

Anyway, it's time. Time to hang up the old stethoscope. Time to move on. I've seen the faces of the people on the square. I don't know how they found out I'd been trying to help her. I prefer to keep the curtains drawn. They've been taken down now of course. I see some of them when I visit Mark's corner shop and that busybody – Carol is it? – who's organising things. She seems to make a beeline for me if she sees me. I've watched what they've done to the square. But it's better to hide.

Though maybe there's one thing I need to do first.

Sipping coffee and staring at the bound piled-up copies of the *BMJ* and *Lancet,* I think how you read those, you get "CME points", and points always mean prizes, well a positive annual appraisal at least. Reading the journals and keeping up to date has always been a bit of a chore, but the annual round of appraisals kept everyone on their toes. The requirement of an annual appraisal with its commitment to Continuing Medical Education or "CME" had been introduced some years ago to

155

ensure that all General Practitioners kept up to date, and if I recall it right, was specifically aimed at the older generation of General Practitioners like me. It was what those "high heidyins" of the medical profession had wanted, slipping back into the old Glasgow jargon without thinking. I remember that back then I, and many of my contemporaries, had thought that the new regulations were specifically aimed at what they called "Us oldies" but many of them didn't really understand much of what was being published in those journals, so like everyone else we had stuck with just reading the editorials, the letters and the obituaries.

As I sip my coffee I'm thinking, how retiral, they say opens a door to new possibilities. Well, here I am in the old house where I've lived and mostly worked as a GP for well over thirty years; I mean that's all I've ever wanted to be, a family practitioner, and here in this house is where it all started some thirty-five years ago. I'd like to think it's all come to a perfect end, but it feels tainted somehow.

I ran the original small practice from the house on the edge of the square using one front downstairs room as the surgery and another room as the waiting room. My wife and one other lady were the receptionist and practice manager respectively. The house is one of those old Victorian double-fronted houses, two large bay windows, two large reception rooms that we used for the practice, a decent-sized room at the back for me and my wife, and a big spacious kitchen.

I think about some of the people I've seen over the years, and the stories I could tell would easily fill a large volume. Foreign bodies inserted into the wrong orifice, vacuum-cleaner injuries, sexually-transmitted diseases, unwanted or unexpected pregnancies, and other comedic and tragic stories. Yup, I could write a book, maybe semi-autobiographical, add a bit of humour; it could be a fun project for my retired life, might even become a bestseller, maybe call it *The Square Doctor*.

My single-handed practice itself was swallowed up some years ago and incorporated into the new much larger GP Practice in the nearby purpose-built Health Centre; but for many years me and my wife have continued to live in the house, where I run a small clinic a couple of times a week with the blessing of the Group Practice; but now it's time to retire and move to one of the smaller villages in Kent. The new house has been selected and purchased, and the house in the square has been sold, and in the next week we are due to move out. The movers have been booked, contracts exchanged, and new curtains and carpets have been measured up and ordered.

I trained in Glasgow in the late sixties, a time of gang wars, followed by "The Ice Cream Wars", when stabbings and the "Glasgow Kiss" were the order of the day.

After completing my studies and the obligatory House Jobs plus a further two years as a Senior House Officer in medicine and a couple of other specialties, I'd started my formal GP training with a six-month rotation in the A&E department of the Glasgow Royal, which was a bit like being the Sheriff in Deadwood or Tombstone, and was enough to equip any doctor for any emergency. This was then followed by six-month rotation at the Royal Hospital for Children and then a further six months at "Rottenrow", the old maternity hospital in the east end of Glasgow, officially known as "The Royal Maternity Hospital", where I'd distinguished myself as being the first junior doctor to faint at a Caesarean Section. Those latter two jobs fulfilled both my Paediatric and Obstetric requirements for General Practice.

157

I recall that fainting episode with a smile. In the early hours of the morning, I'd been called up to assist at a Caesarean Section after having watched and dozed through *Alien* in the Doctor's Mess. I'd walked into the operating theatre which was dark except for the OR lamp shining on the patient's abdomen, just as the Senior Registrar delivered the baby via the abdominal incision – Alien – Baby – Alien – Baby – I was just too tired to figure out the difference and suffered what was known in Glasgow as the "Moving Pavement Syndrome" and hit the floor.

The General Practice end of the rotation was carried out in the Shettlestone area of Glasgow, a deprived area of the city which at the time had almost a 100% unemployment rate, compounded by high alcohol consumption and drug use, with the job itself being more of a social worker than a Medical Practitioner. An additional role I found myself landed with was the provision of medical care at the Bar-L or officially HM Prison Barlinnie a pretty thankless task, that frequently involved knife wounds, drug overdose and attempted suicide. The Victorian prison was a dark brooding place, straight out of a Dickensian novel, and the guys that filled it, well that's another tale and that could fill another book.

A final twelve-month period in General Practice was carried out in the leafy south side of Glasgow, a middle-class suburb, where I dealt with bored housewives, urinary tract infections, and a whole range of those so-called middle-class ailments. This all nicely rounded off the training programme. Unfortunately, I reminded myself that back then, there was absolutely no training in Mental Health or Mental Welfare; my generation of General Practitioners had absolutely no idea about any of that at all. And maybe that was my downfall.

I moved south to this area, where I took over this particular single-handed practice in the square. Then came the NHS Reorganisation, swiftly followed by the Shipman episode, the subsequent enquiries and the fall out. This resulted in the belief that many single-handed practitioners were acting not only in isolation, but unsupervised, and unregulated in their activities, and the majority failing to keep up to date which would nowadays not be tolerated. Despite protests, from the many GPs countrywide, as well as many of their patients, they were all "encouraged"– well those were the new Regulators' words – to move into larger group practices. Simply put, it was either that, or have all their patients transferred over to the new large all-singing all-dancing, now fully supervised Group Practices, mostly sited in specifically designed health centres. Despite the complaints from many of my patients, I had gracefully moved into the new purpose-built Health Centre where I and fifteen other General Practitioners and all their support staff provided a full range of family services, developed their own and nurse-led specialist clinics, and encouraged patients to attend for a health "MOT".

Despite my initial misgivings it had all worked out well, and I managed to keep control of my own patient list, and with the blessing of both the managers of the Group Practice, and the "Regulators" I could still see a few patients at my home, where I was permitted to run a weekly satellite clinic, as did many of my single-handed colleagues, who had cooperated with the new regulations. This was of course done with the full agreement, of firstly the Healthcare Commission, and more latterly with the Infamous Care Quality Commission or the CQC, as they were now universally known.

Despite the move to the health centre, the Frequent Flyers, the heartsink patients, and those that just wanted to chat to the "Good" Doctor still preferred to turn up at my weekly clinic on the square. These patients clearly felt that the individual consultation process in the "Good" Doctor's House in the Square was much less hurried, calmer, and the "Good" Doctor would always give them much, much more time to address their many medical, social and welfare problems.

Joanne was one amongst many of those patients who had repeatedly attended the "Good Doctor's House in the square", with a variety of nebulous symptoms that had included, weight loss, sleep problems, abdominal pain, panic attacks, recurrent headaches, and a constant sensation of fluttering in the chest. She was always accompanied by her mum though I saw Joanne alone. I always asked if she wanted her mother present. She always declined and you have to respect the patient's wishes and their confidentiality. Joanne was of course of an age where she was considered an independent adult.

Guiltily, to my everlasting regret, is that I didn't fully understand what those symptoms really represented; maybe I should have delved deeper into her background, maybe addressed her worries, delved more into her relationships with her friends and probable boyfriends, and why she was missing school. Possibly referred her for a Mental Health assessment, and organised Social Welfare visits, or even referred her for a formal Social Care assessment, but I didn't. I will have to carry that guilt and regret. As I've said before I really wasn't trained in Mental Health Welfare and my understanding of safeguarding was sketchy at best. Could or should I have done better? I simply put her symptoms down to teenage anxiety and naively assumed that this was due to exam worry, and girlfriend and boyfriend issues. I really should have done better.

Sadly, it's been a year since Joanne's death, and I'll have to carry that responsibility, and the remorse and regret have not disappeared. Could I have done anything different, should I have arranged for her to have a Mental Health Assessment, sought out Social Services? Would that have altered the outcome? I couldn't really say for certain, and I'm sure nobody else could. I mean as doctors we don't have a crystal ball to look into the future, but maybe a timely referral to a mental health team would have helped, possibly, possibly changed the outcome. A couple of days after her death I saw her name booked in for an appointment. It had been scheduled for the week after she died. It turned out she had called and asked to see me; my receptionist seemed to think she had sounded agitated, asking to see me that day, but she only said this after the terrible event that was to transpire, so maybe it was her own guilt speaking. Joanne was offered an appointment for the following week. I recall seeing her name and crossing it out.

Should I have seen her? Would she have said what she intended to do, a cry for help? But like I said – none of us have crystal balls. We can't ever know what someone might or will do. I visited the family the day it happened, crossed the square to offer my assistance. When you learn that someone has taken their own life, it always stays with you. Even when you're trained to offer support you can still be lost for the right thing to say. And when you later find out why, because of a photograph, the true horror of a wasted young life hits and has a way of keep on hitting you.

Looking around the now partially empty old consulting room I ask myself, "Is this why as a consequence, I've now shut the clinic at my home, sold the house on Station Square and am now moving; hanging up my stethoscope? I'll now have to move on like everyone else, and anyway retiral beckons."

Standing up from my old comfortable chair, I adjust my black tie; it doesn't matter what they think of me, I have to do this before I leave. I might sit, I might hover at the back but if anyone asks, I'll tell them the truth: I am not God. I did my best, didn't I?

It's time to attend young Joanne's Memorial because maybe something good might come from this terrible tragedy. We can only hope.

Epilogue

October 13th

Holden Caulfield was sixteen, an age you will never reach. The age I was when I tried to do what you did.

It wasn't a failed attempt. I never got that far. But I would have, I had it all planned. Because I didn't do it, I am here now and everyone is listening.

"When Joanne died, she was reading *The Catcher in the Rye*. Some of you may have read it. It deals with a young boy growing up. The first thing I remember about Holden Caulfield was his sense of rebellion, but also his feelings of alienation. He wanted to save children from falling off a cliff. It doesn't mean literally, it symbolises the loss of innocence and the transition into an adult world. It seems we are we always in such a rush to get there and sometimes our minds get caught between two worlds – between that of a child and that of an adult." I make sure I look at the children as I say this part. "I realise now it's all about perspective. When we're young we don't realise that the small things seem so much bigger than they really are. We don't have the sense of perspective that comes with age, but... *You can't afford to lose a minute.* It's another quote from the book. And it's so true. In our innocence we don't consider the consequences of our actions. It might be an old book but people don't change from one century to the next – do they? Except Holden Caulfield would never have known the kind of world you all live in, let alone known the damage that a single photograph could have done." There's a murmur, an uneasy shifting and shuffling of feet because they would all have seen it – the younger ones. I look at Miss Dawson, your form tutor.

"It's easy to think there's no way out," I say, "but there

163

always is. Because that's what happened to me. I spoke to someone. Someone who made me see that in time *everything passes.* No matter how terrible something seems – it will pass, it will get better. I could never have imagined that. That's why I do the work I do, raise the money I do for charity and why I wrote my story. I wrote it five years later in the hope that if it touches one life, changes one mind, I will have made a difference. But this isn't about me, or headlines," I look directly at the press, "it's about lifting stigma. It's not a crime to do what Joanne did. It's not been a crime since 1961. So, I urge all of you not to say "committed suicide" like it is a crime. You commit murder, you commit adultery – Joanne took her life. She made a choice and the sad part – the saddest most tragic part of all – is it could have been prevented." I resist the urge to look at the boy standing at the back by the gate because if there's one thing I know above all else – this is not the place for blame. Not here. Not now.

"Look around you… go on. Look at how many people live here on this square or go to your school. We have people here today of all ages, and we all have our own demons to fight. We wouldn't be human if we didn't feel low or afraid or alone, but all you have to do is reach out, to one another. A family member, a friend, a neighbour. There's also a dedicated phone line that you'll find on the leaflets that have been handed out. And Miss Dawson will tell you more about that.

It might sound too simple but talking saved me. Even when whatever you're dealing with seems insurmountable there is always a solution. For Joanne Wilson, who was bright, popular and I wish I had known her – it's too late. She's become a statistic because on average, around five young people take their lives each day in the UK." I stop for a moment to let the enormity of this settle, before I resume. "I was where Joanne was, maybe not the same

164

street but in my case, it was the same town. Maybe not for the same reason but I was her and no one was going to stop me… I would have been another statistic but thank God I found my courage – to tell someone how I was feeling and I got help. I learned it's true – everything does pass."

And the part I don't say. I knew it would be someone who loved me who would find me. Like they found you. Thank God it didn't happen. I look at your family and I know you didn't mean for it to be that way, but they too must live with those consequences.

There's a ripple of sound, soft stifled sobs and gentle murmurs and I look along all the faces, not just the young. "That's why things have to change and that's why I came. And why Carol Sargeant and Miss Dawson are going to talk to you about measures being put in place in schools. I know it might take more than that but we all have to start somewhere. Any of you heard that message they play on some trains – *if you see something that doesn't look right, report it – see it, say it, sort it.* There's a soft rumble of sound and young faces smile in recognition. "Well, that's what we have to do with one another. If you think someone's not okay, ask them, listen and if you're still worried – tell an adult. Because if there's one thing I never want to do again," I look out as I say it, "it's to stand here and read the words from another young person's diary knowing it's too late for them."

I hold my hands out and stop them applauding, and ask for a minute's hush while they all think about you – Joanne Wilson. I'm still clutching your diary when I go back to my seat and Miss Dawson stands up, signalling to Carol who will speak after her.

Miss Dawson is outlining all the new procedures… a string of words and phrases: intimate image abuse, nude and semi-nude images, that while it isn't illegal to take intimate photos or share them with a boyfriend or girlfriend, it is illegal to share them on social media without consent. She also talks about cyberbullying and those dreadful sites that encourage children to actually play games with their own lives.

Carol is up next and says she is working closely with the charity and wants to set up a support group and Miss Dawson will pass on details to them at school. She speaks so eloquently about standing up to bullies, not being a victim. I watch the small group at the back as Carol speaks. I think about Jack and what I said to him.

They're all applauding loudly now and I see the proud look on Carol's face when they thank her. I know how she suffered – bullying comes in many forms and look how she made this happen. She's fighting for the right to stand up and speak out, not hold it in. Suicide is not a crime, nor should it be a taboo subject.

The last person to speak is Raymond Tiller, the vicar, good friends with your mum and dad, though today is not that kind of memorial but it feels right somehow that we end with him. That we celebrate the life that was snuffed out far too soon. Because it's too easy to get stuck at the end, at the last part when it's such a small part of a whole life – even a short one. People are asked to think of happy memories and share them afterwards.

Now back in my seat, as Raymond Tiller finishes his part, I look at the back.

I had urged Jack to come but I wasn't sure he would.

He's standing apart from his aunt and uncle now.

His mum and dad didn't come. He said they wouldn't.

This is not about blame. It took a lot of guts for him to be here.

166

It never was about blame.

Something Jack said still haunts me. He said his favourite TV show is *Dr Who* and how you'd watched it together. He said you liked quotes from books and TV shows and there was one from *Dr Who* that you kept repeating. He said it was – *we're all just stories in the end.* And he'd looked right at me. "Is that all she is now?"

How do you even answer that?

And there was the other thing he said. He told me if he'd known, if he had any idea what his actions would do, he would never have done it. He'd sobbed then, a pitiful sad hollow sob that scooped me out. "I never told her I was sorry."

"Tell her now."

I remember the way he looked at me when I said that. He did a stupid, some might say cruel thing, but he needs support too. That's why I reached out to him, so he never has to feel what you did – never has to think there's no way out. "Say it to her. Whisper it, write it, think it, doesn't matter how you say it, say it, Jack. And I know from what people tell me about her – she'd forgive you, Jack. I forgive you."

It's only for a moment and I probably imagined it but as I look back across at Jack, I think I see someone holding his hand – it's a trick of the light, a shadow made by the silver birch and a moment later it's gone. I know we see the things we want to see but right now I want him to feel forgiven – whatever he did no one could have known you'd do what you did.

It's only after they've all gone and I stand alone at the edge of the railings of the communal garden, under the silver birch, I realise that as each of them went home, back to their own troubles, they all took a part of you with them. But I hope after all the nice things people said – it's the good parts; the best parts they remember. I don't want people to get stuck at the end, they need to move past that.

People need to remember you as the bright girl you were. The girl who had hopes and dreams and plans to go to uni and a whole life ahead of her. They all need to remember you like that, Joanne. You could have been so much more than just a story or a memory… the saddest part is that's the only way you exist now.

I walk to the gate, look along the four rows of houses that face the gardens, think about all the people I met today. I'd talked to so many and then watched them walk back to their lives feeling maybe they were walking a little lighter, a little less burdened. You can hope. Your family did look over at number 11 but only for a moment. I think Elizabeth wanted to invite them in to hers but they said no. I get it, how hard that would be. Someone said they think it will be up for sale soon, I know the current tenants have plans to move back to Italy. I wonder whose home it will be next?

I watched them – the Wilsons – walk away, maybe back to the tube or their car. I'm not sure they will ever get closure, will they?

As I leave the garden and head towards the alleyway, I pull my coat tighter and see the curtain twitch at number 4. Maisie is standing at the window raising a glass of something cloudy.

I know that this time last year you did something you could never come back from and not so long ago – that could so easily have been me. But the words in your diary stay with me. I think they will always stay with me. You talked about a TV show you loved and how you were reminded of being that little girl who wanted to be noticed.

168

I picture the very last words you wrote. And I'd like to think that's what today was really about.

Taking the sourest lemons life had to offer and making lemonade.

Afterword

Before we reach the discussion page, I want to talk to you about Joanne's diary. We decided as a group to include some of her diary as a way of giving Joanne a voice in the story. We wanted and hoped we have captured some of her mindset. All of the fictional diary extracts start with a quote that we felt was relevant, most from *The Catcher in the Rye*. You will see some at the end of her diary extract typeset in bold. What I want to tell you all is that these **were the actual words found in diaries of real teenagers who took their own lives**. I want you all to think about, maybe re-read, some of these lines. At the end of the book, you will find references to these stories. They are here because they were put in the public domain by their families to raise awareness about suicide.

Thank you for reading this book. Please share it with others. Because this is a serious subject matter, we urge you to work through the discussion points with your family and friends. If you feel any of the things any of the characters in this story feel, especially Joanne, please reach out to someone. There is always hope. At the end of this book are contact details for how to get help – don't face this alone.

Debz Hobbs-Wyatt

Discussion Points

1. What do you think about Joanne Wilson as a character? We only meet her through diary extracts and other people's memories. Do you feel as if you understand her and what she did? Do you have a diary?

2. Do you think Joanne should have slept with Jack? How do you think you would react to that kind of pressure from a boyfriend? Should Adrian, the friend she told, have done more to help?

3. Do you think Joanne should have sent the semi-nude photograph to her boyfriend? Is she at fault for sending it or is Jack at fault for sharing it? How do you think you would react in a situation like that as either the one being asked to send a photo or the one who does the asking? Has this book made you think differently about that?

4. What do you think of Jack Henderson? Was it right to show a mate the photograph? Do you think, after what happened, he deserves to be forgiven?

5. What do you think about social media where a photo can "go viral"? Should there be more in place to try to stop this happening or is it all down to personal freedom of choice? Do you blame cyberbullying on the phone companies or the phone users? In the days of some of our older characters, the technology would not have made it possible. So, what do you think about not letting teenagers have phones?

6. Do you think the schools should have better ways of

dealing with bullying. What measures are you aware of?

7. Is there a well-being room in your school? Is it used? Do you think if Joanne had talked to one of her teachers, someone trained to understand the dangers of the internet or even the pressures being put on young people, the story might have had a different outcome?

8. From what you know about Joanne, do you think, if she had talked to someone, in school or on the square, especially her own parents, it could have prevented her from taking her own life?

9. Who, out of all the characters who lived on the square, do you think could have helped Joanne the most when she was feeling the way she was?

10. Joanne writes in her diary that there is **no way out**. She writes "FAILED". That is three days before she takes her life. Do you think there was a way out? Have you ever felt there wasn't? Who did or would you talk to?

11. Who, of all the characters – Jada, Maisie, Elizabeth, Piper, Matt, Edith, Calcutta, Adrian, Danny, Carol, Dimitri (and Lucinda), Schu, Abigail or the doctor would you most like to sit down and have a coffee with?

12. What have your learned about the issues other people have to deal with from reading this book? Does it make you want to understand other people more from seeing how people have to deal with things? Think about the things the different characters deal with maybe jot some down for discussion. For example: Maisie and her

hoarding, why do you think people do that? What about Piper's betrayal and how that was represented in the media? Carol, even as an old lady, makes a stand to help victims of bullying because she herself had an abusive husband. What about our gay couple and how they thought they were being snubbed because of homophobic beliefs or the MMA fighter on the sex register because of a girl who lied about her age, is that right or wrong?

13. Should the "good" doctor have done more? It might interest you to know that this character was written by a retired doctor so he does know how "the system" works. Do doctors need a better system in place to better recognise and treat young people with mental health issues? If you were feeling the way Joanne was, would you have spoken to your doctor? Or a parent? Friend?

14. What do you think is the biggest message to come from reading *Making Lemonade*? And do you think it will help lift the stigma on suicide – especially in young people by encouraging people to talk openly about it and more importantly about their feelings so they can get help.

15. Who do you think Joanne would be now if she had not taken her own life? How about writing a new diary entry for her on October 14th the day after she chose, instead, to live... what would she do next? Who would she talk to? What will she become in life if only she had a second chance?

The Real Diary Extracts

These words were taken from real diaries by young people who took their own lives. Their families bravely allowed their words to be made public in the hope they would highlight the very real need to understand and dispel the stigma surrounding suicide. Trigger warning: if you choose to read their stories, be aware that these are real stories about real teenagers who felt there was no way out. If only they had been able to reach out to someone.

We'd like to dedicate this special book to children and adults who have taken their own lives.

We thank the families for allowing this to be in the public domain and a special thanks to Megan Meier's mother, Tina Meier, for agreeing to let us use perhaps the most pertinent line from Megan's diary written the same night she was a victim of cyberbullying. It sounds like something Joanne Wilson could have said.

Megan Meier, died by suicide aged 13 (three weeks before her 14th birthday).

You're the kind of boy a girl would kill herself over.
https://www.meganmeierfoundation.org/

Izzy Dix, died by suicide aged 14.

Another piece of me chiselled away by their cruel remarks and perceptions… I give up
https://www.theguardian.com/society/2013/dec/12/school girl-killed-herself-bullied-inquest

Jonah Habedank, died by suicide aged 18. His final journal entry read "Tell My Story"…

...*a quitter, a failure, and a coward*
https://www.unilad.com/news/world-news/suicide-teenager-cincinatti-final-journal-entry-795333-20250213

Alexandra Valoras, died by suicide aged 17. Unlike Joanne the bright, happy person everyone saw was in stark contrast to what she had been writing in her diary.

I'm so lost, I'm so hopeless, I am so worthless…
(one of several quotes taken from Alexandra's diary).
https://www.cbsnews.com/news/a-lost-girls-diary-alexandra-valoras/

Sadly, if you look online, you will find many many more stories like these that should never have happened. All suicide is preventable. It doesn't end the chance of life getting worse but what it does do is eliminates the possibility of it ever getting better. Remember, whatever you're feeling – *this too will pass* and it's really okay to seek help – **talk to someone.**

PREVENTION
OF YOUNG SUICIDE

Suicide is the biggest killer of young people under the age of thirty-five in the UK.

PAPYRUS aims to reduce the number of young people who take their own lives by breaking down the stigma around suicide and equipping people with the skills to recognise and respond to suicidal behaviour.

HOPELINE247 is the charity's confidential helpline service providing practical advice and support to young people with thoughts of suicide and anyone concerned about a young person who may have thoughts of suicide.

HOPELINE247 is staffed by trained professionals, offering a telephone, text and email service.

For practical, confidential suicide prevention help and advice, please contact PAPYRUS HOPELINE247 on 0800 068 4141, text 88247 or email pat@papyrus-uk.org

Meet The Authors

Character names also listed

Debz Hobbs-Wyatt (Charity worker, Joanne's Diary)

Debz Hobbs-Wyatt is a full-time writer and editor. She has had over thirty short stories published in collections, amassed shortlists and competition wins, including being nominated for the prestigious US Pushcart Prize, on the short list of the Commonwealth Short Story Prize and winner of the inaugural Bath Short Story Award. *While No One Was Watching*, her debut novel, was published by Parthian Books in 2013. Her short story collection *Because Sometimes Something Extraordinary Happens* was published in July 2019 and her new novel *If Crows Could Talk* was published by Walela Books in October 2024. She is represented by Camilla Shestopal from Shesto Literary.

Lynn Sansom (Jada)

Lynn Sansom, originally a professional florist, has recently honed her creative skills in pursuing her passion for writing. But it was her passion for reading that lead her to meet Debz through the local library where she was encouraged to join the Canvey Writers. Lynn chose to write about Jada the teacher as she has experience working as a teaching assistant. Lynn is now in the process of writing her memoirs for her two sons: Lee and Perry. Her hobbies are Ballroom and Latin dancing. This is her first published work.

Margaret Potter (Maisie)

Margaret Potter has had sixteen short stories published in *Woman's Weekly*, one reproduced in their yearbook 2014. Two short stories in *Yours* magazine. Picture script stories in *Postman Pat* magazine and one in their annual. Her stories for children have been published in D.C. Thomson publications and in 2014, she won first prize in Penzance Literary Festival "Be a Write Pirate" competition. She was thrilled to have a story for children printed in braille for the RNIB, therefore reaching another audience. Margaret enjoys the lively writing discussions with all the members of Canvey Writers.

Anastasia Ho Chee (Elizabeth)

Anastasia was born in Greece, the youngest of three children, first generation of refugees from the Black Sea of displaced Greeks, known as Pontic. She loves writing little stories about her experiences although none of these have been published. Anastasia has been a member of Canvey Writers for a few years where she has met some amazingly talented people. After forty years in Nursing, she believes it is time to write her memoir and share stories about her family. Her house was always open to people who needed somewhere to crash for the night or taste her grandmother's amazing cooking. She chose the name Elizabeth because it was the name of her mother's little sister who passed at the age of three during the displacement.

Paris Walker (Piper)

Paris Walker is currently a student at the University of Brighton, getting her bachelor's degree in English Literature and Creative Writing. She is currently a short story and flash fiction writer, and hopes to one day publish her current work in progress, *The Pear*. She loves to read anything by Ali Hazelwood and loves a good gothic thriller! *Making Lemonade* includes her first piece of published work; she has been a member of the Canvey Writers since 2022.

P.A. Westgate (Matt)

P. A. Westgate, Paul, lets his imagination run wild through short-story writing. One of the original members of Canvey Writers he was first published in 2016, with the latest in 2024. Some of Paul's writing can be found at www.cafelitmagazine.co.uk. He was a prize-winner at the Southend Festival of Performing Arts in 2022 and 2024. In addition to writing, Paul enjoys an eclectic mix of activities including reading, singing, the Arts and cocktails. He lives quietly in his native Essex where he tries, with varying degrees of success, to keep his house and garden tidy.

Anna Cundall (Edith)

Anna loves reading and met Debz at her local library, in summer of 2023 and was encouraged to join Canvey Writers. She was inspired to write her story about Edith after a stay in hospital with her own heart problems. Anna worked with people with health issues and their families. She especially liked listening to older people talk about their early lives. Anna cared for her own mum who had dementia, and understands the challenges of losing a loved one to dementia. Anna's interests are creative arts, crafts, social history and of course reading. This is her first published work.

Dave Traer (Calcutta)
Dave has been a member of Canvey Writers for over eight years. He has two longer pieces, both of which remain unfinished, but his true love is writing short stories. Some have been published in print and via the CaféLit website. He was born and bred in London's East End, moving to Canvey after his marriage. Most of his works are character driven and can, as in this case, sit beyond his comfort zone. Years of working, as an electrician, on countless building sites, has given him a pool of character types to choose from. He hopes that the reader enjoys his depiction of Calcutta Drake.

Colin Wyatt (Adrian)
Colin has spent his working life as a children's illustrator, which has included designing the visual concept for *The Poddington Peas* which became an animated series shown regularly on BBC Television. He also illustrated such well-known characters as *Noddy* and *Thomas the Tank Engine*. He worked for Walt Disney Productions for more than twenty years, producing artwork for Disney publications such as annuals and weekly comics. Colin's writing career began in 2011 when he wrote and illustrated *The Jet-Set*, a picture book series published by Paws n Claws Publishing, about four super-hero animal characters that help wild animals in trouble. Colin's latest book, which, again, he has both written and illustrated, is *Who will be my Friend?* published by Chapeltown Books.

Peter Sandling (Danny)
Peter has been writing short stories and poetry for a number of years. He likes to include subject matter from all areas of life and is particularly interested in people's reactions to specific situations and tries to incorporate these in his work. He has a varied interest in literature and is a member of a crime reading

group. He used to run a small, informal writing group fortnightly at Canvey Library. He was very pleased to have a short story published in Cafélit. Peter is married with two adult sons. He says that all family members are artistically and musically talented but his only contribution during musical get-togethers is his proficiency on the washboard and paper and comb. Peter is a keen bowls player and enjoys every moment of his retirement.

Diane Rust (Carol)

Diane is a relatively new member of Canvey Writers. By chance she met Debz whilst visiting Canvey Island Library just over two years ago. Following a conversation and some encouragement to join. Diane became a member. She recalled the fun she had composing poems to suit special family occasions and had also enjoyed writing dissertations whilst studying Classical Civilisations during her Open University course. She has always enjoyed the Writers' meetings and is delighted that this will be her first piece of published writing. Her hobbies include art, floral art, creating and maintaining bonsai trees and all things horticultural.

John Bamford (Dimitri)

John Bamford was born on the cusp. At the stroke of midnight, between the 14th and 15th of August That is an interesting fact not many people know! He likes to tinker; to take things apart and put them back together which is why he now lives in a house with lots of things – especially old watches. One man's junk is another man's treasure! As for writing, while his sensible day job was an engineer, in the 1960s/70s he wrote song lyrics and had a number of poems published. He is currently working on a couple of old-fashioned detective novels. You will find him working with Canvey Writers' founder, Debz, every other Friday in the local library... plotting!

Vicky Jacobson (Schu)

Vicky is a retired legal secretary with two grown-up children. She discovered a love of books at an early age when her grandfather read her bedtime stories as a small child and was reading them for herself by the time she started school. She has always wanted

180

to write and joined Canvey Writers when it first started in the hope of finding inspiration. This resulted in two of her short stories being published on the CaféLit site and she was absolutely delighted when both were picked for the "Best of" anthology for their respective years. She also produced a story for the Group's earlier collaboration published in 2017.

Julie Kendall (Abigail)

Julie has been an active member of our group since it started ten years ago. She likes writing short stories and poems. Most of these are about relationships and love! She enjoyed writing Abigail's part in the story, although lonely she had willpower to make the best of her life and made friends. Julie has an allotment and had lots of strawberries this year. She loves gardening also belongs to an art group and enjoys walking. She belonged to an amateur dramatic group for sixteen years.

Henry Lewi (The "Good" Doctor)

Henry is a retired surgeon and member of the Canvey Writers. He is a regular contributor to the CaféLit site run by Bridge House Publishing and has had over thirty short stories published. Additionally, he is a monthly Columnist to the Essex Magazine *Over The Edge*. Henry has recently had two collections of short stories published by Bridge House Publishing and Chapeltown Books titled *Once We Were Heroes* and *From The Beginning To The End*.

Acknowledgements

A huge thanks to all the members of **Canvey Writers** for their hard work, passion and dedication to this project; including the other members who have helped by offering their feedback throughout the process.

Thanks to **Gill James** at **Bridge House Publishing** for agreeing to take on this special book and to her husband, **Martin James,** the designer, for finding the perfect cover and for creating what you are holding in your hand. Thanks also to **Hannah Retallick,** for her editorial input, catching the things we missed!

A massive thanks to the team at the charity: **PAPYRUS – Prevention of Young Suicide** – and in particular to **Peter Holland** (Dutch) who gave this book its first standing ovation! Their guidelines taught us all just how much it matters how suicide is represented in the media, including fiction.

And finally, a special thanks to **YOU** for buying this book. Please help us keep the conversation going about suicide; to lift the stigmas and to stop it being a taboo subject. We don't want there to be a Joanne Wilson on your street... or a need for making lemonade.

Like to Read More Work Like This?

Then sign up to our mailing list and download our free collection of short stories, *Magnetism*. Sign up now to receive this free e-book and also to find out about all of our new publications and offers.

Sign up here:
   http://eepurl.com/gbpdVz

Please Leave a Review

Reviews are so important to writers. Please take the time to review this book. A couple of lines is fine.

Reviews help the book to become more visible to buyers. Retailers will promote books with multiple reviews.

This in turn helps us to sell more books… And then we can afford to publish more books like this one.

Leaving a review is very easy.

Go to https://amzn.to/4hpbd9G, scroll down the left-hand side of the Amazon page and click on the "Write a customer review" button.

Other Writing by Canvey Writers

Tales from the Upper Room

edited by Janice Gilbert, Debz Hobbs-Wyatt and Gini Scanlan

Poems and Short Stories by the Canvey Writers, St Nicholas Group, who meet in the upstairs room…

You will be wowed by the dark tales: a modern day Little Red Riding Hood – as you have never seen her before. You will wait for the Reaper to come and you'll encounter ghosts in different forms. You will laugh at how Mavis and cat, Cuddles, and a glass of Lambrusco manage to start World War III, and how a job search lands aging Mr Montegoo the perfect job. You will read about war, about hate, and about love. You will encounter the power of what-if moments, love that endures, lovers that got away and the effect of the choices we make in life.

Proceeds from the sale of this book will be donated to Havens Hospices

Order from Amazon:

Paperback: ISBN 978-1-907335-19-8

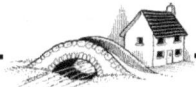

Once We Were Heroes
by Henry Lewi

Where do the gods of Olympus do their shopping?

Do the Old Gods live amongst us, and if so where? And which jobs do they do? Where do the Old Gods shop, or do they do it online? Which football clubs do they support? When Angels are sent down to Earth, how do they get home? How did Vampires cope with Lockdown during the pandemic? And finally, are Extra-Terrestrials dangerous, or do they just want to speak to us?

"Henry Lewi writes with confidence and with imagination. The story about the gods moving to North London provided an interesting opportunity to comment on modern times. The Pandemic features in many of the items in the collection."
(Amazon)

Order from Amazon:

Paperback: ISBN 978-1-914199-82-0
eBook: ISBN 978-1-914199-83-7

Because Sometimes Something Extraordinary Happens

by Debz Hobbs-Wyatt

Seventeen short stories by Debz Hobbs-Wyatt from over a decade of competition wins and shortlistings.

Meet a mixture of beguiling narrators, from seven-year-old Leonardo Renoir Hope trying to change the past so his dad doesn't die, and George and his carrot-growing friends on an east London allotment waiting for the world to end, to Amy Fisher who realises that her husband, after his sudden death, is not who she thinks he is… but who is the other Mrs Fisher? This one adds a touch of medical horror to the mix.

All of the stories are about ordinary people when extraordinary things happen to them.

"What an inspiring collection of short stories and it is no surprise to find they are award-winning." *(Amazon)*

Order from Amazon:

Paperback: ISBN 978-1-907335-69-3
eBook: ISBN 978-1-907335-70-9

If Crows Could Talk
by Debz Hobbs-Wyatt

George Tucker and April Jefferson have never met but they share a secret.

Born the same day fifty years apart, in the same town in Florida, both are battling demons. George is African-American - now living in Atlanta, having run from Jim Crow - only it seems you can't outrun the past. April is a white teenager terrified she will end up like her mother.

George's story is set over fifty years, April's over a single year... yet their destinies are tied up together. They must meet... but how is the troubled teenager April the key to unlocking the secrets of George's past?

Find out in the gripping *If Crows Could Talk* by award-winning literary writer Debz Hobbs-Wyatt.

"Fab-u-lous. A brilliant read, it did make me cry.It should be up there with the best sellers." *(Amazon)*

Order from Amazon:

Paperback: ISBN 978-1-914199-74-5
eBook: ISBN 978-1-914199-75-2

Other Publications by Bridge House

Something Very Human
by Hannah Retallick

This collection takes the reader on a journey through life, from
the innocence of young voices to the reflections of those
seeking meaning as they look back at the paths they've taken.

Each story captures the very essence of being human. The
characters tackle everyday challenges, face inner struggles,
navigate familial relationships and friendships, fall in love and
out of love, process grief, and reflect on the beautiful fragility
of it all.

Something Very Human is the debut short story collection from
award-winning writer, Hannah Retallick.

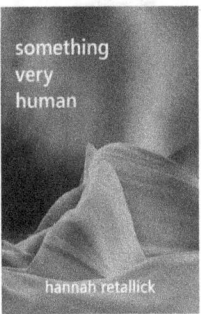

"This was quite a collection of unputdownable short stories.
Except I needed to take a break after each one to savour the
impact and not move on too quickly!" *(Amazon)*

Order from Amazon:

Paperback: ISBN 978-1-914199-76-9
eBook: ISBN 978-1-914199-77-6

Good News...?

edited by Debz Hobbs-Wyatt and Gill James

Oh, be careful what you wish for.

One person's good news might be someone else's bad news. And if you do get what you wished for you might not be getting what you need. Or, if you're slightly more fortunate, you may no longer have anything to grumble about. These stories challenge the notion of what is good news and yet leave us still a little optimistic.

An amazing group of writers set the record straight in Bridge House's anthology *Good News....?*

Order from Amazon:

Paperback: ISBN 978-1-914199-88-2
eBook: ISBN 978-1-914199-89-9

www.ingramcontent.com/pod-product-compliance
Lightning Source LLC
Chambersburg PA
CBHW061205170626
46809CB00003B/1254